The Christmas Box

TONI BLAKE

All rights reserved.

No part of this publication may be sold, copied, distributed, reproduced or transmitted in any form or by any means, mechanical or digital, including photocopying and recording or by any information storage and retrieval system without the prior written permission of both the publisher, Oliver Heber Books and the author, Toni Blake, except in the case of brief quotations embodied in critical articles and reviews.

PUBLISHER'S NOTE: This is a work of fiction. Names, characters, places, and incidents either are the product of the author's imagination or are used fictitiously. Any resemblance to actual persons, living or dead, business establishments, events, or locales is entirely coincidental.

The Christmas Box Copyright 2024 © Toni Herzog

Cover design by Dar Albert at Wicked Smart Designs

Published by Oliver-Heber Books

0 9 8 7 6 5 4 3 2 1

To Jacqueline Daher, whose brainstorming help and feedback truly helped shape this book. I so appreciate your devotion, care, and emotional investment in my work!

Dear Reader,

I'm so pleased to present to you The Christmas Box. When I wrote my last book, The Wedding Box, I was sure it was a stand-alone project. But when I decided to make my next book a Christmas story, with a similar vibe, it only made sense to call it The Christmas Box and use that title as the initial seed of inspiration for the story. And—voila—a series was born!

The Box Books are only loosely linked by setting and characters, but are more strongly tied by story elements and tone. All are uplifting and life-affirming, even while they might tug at your heartstrings as characters cope with life's struggles and losses. All the books contain a small miracle or two. And, of course, they're all about a box—or in the case of The Christmas Box, more than one—that have a huge impact on the character's lives.

As a writer, I have long found snippets of my own life sneaking into my books, but that's been especially true of these Box Books. In The Christmas Box, the little town of Winterberry is very loosely based on my hometown of Williamstown, Kentucky, whose Main Street fell on hard times a few decades back but has since burst back to life. If you're ever passing through, stop to check out the shops and restaurants now lining the little street where I shopped as a kid and worked at the library as a teenager. (It's no longer the library, by the way, but that's okay because part of this story is about how places change and evolve over time.)

As with most of my books, this one has ended up very near and dear to my heart. I hope it will be that way for you, as well!

Reader Letter

Sincerely
Toni Blake

Day After Thanksgiving

Lexi

Lugging my new easel sign out into the cold morning twilight, I prop it on the sidewalk. In green chalk I've written: *Grand Opening*.

"Alexandra Louise Hargrove, is it truly happening? Is today really the day?"

I look up to find dear family friend Helen Brightway—once my grandmother's bestie—approaching down the sidewalk. A heavyset woman in her sixties, she wears medical scrubs laden with cartoon Santa faces under her open coat.

"Yes, at last!" I call happily back. "Ten long years in the making!"

"A little early, isn't it?" she asks kiddingly. And rightfully so. It's not even 7a.m. Which might be when the Black Friday shoppers hit the ground running in cities and suburbs, but for shops in a small Kentucky town, our nine o'clock start time today is about as early as we expect people to be out and about.

Even so..."I'm too excited to wait," I tell her. "So I'm just getting everything *extra* ready. And savoring the moment, I suppose."

With that, I turn to face the building I just exited. Erected on Main Street in Winterberry, Kentucky in 1919, the brick structure was originally a bar, then a five-and-dime, and eventually a beauty parlor. For the last thirty years, though, it's sat vacant—until I bought it a few months back. Now, the plate-glass storefront windows announce to passersby that it's become *The Christmas Box*. In smaller letters underneath: *Where Every Day is a Holiday*.

Did I go too far having the lettering painted in red-and-white candy cane stripes? I think not. If you're gonna do something, go all in. The shop display windows are lined with fake snow and an array of small Christmas trees, reindeer, and snowmen. Beyond the window dressing, the building's original mahogany bar remains, now housing the checkout at one end with coffee and cocoa at the other. The rest of the space is filled with antique tables boasting holiday décor and gift items amidst a forest of decorated artificial trees in all shapes and sizes.

As Helen drapes an arm lovingly around my shoulder, we both take in the splendor of my new business. "It's magnificent," she says. "Your mother and grandma would both be very proud."

Her praise warms my heart as I tell her, "That's all I've ever wanted."

The warm little squeeze she gives makes it clear we're

both feeling the loss all over again, just for a minute. Some things never leave you.

"You're gonna do great, honey."

"I hope so. Chet Wheeler says I need to have a banner holiday season to stay solvent through the coming year." Chet is my accountant—Winterberry's *only* accountant, as luck would have it. But he's wisely advised my family on business matters for decades.

The rumble of an engine makes us both turn to see an old red pickup pull to the curb across the street. Old as in vintage-Americana-art old, but it appears well cared for and almost as shiny as new.

"I keep seeing that truck the last few days," I tell Helen. "Any idea who's in it?" In small towns, people make it their business to know such things.

So I'm not surprised when she does. "Travis Hutchins. Tom Hutchins' boy."

Well, *that* part's a surprise. I try not to let it show on my face.

"Didn't you go to school with him?" she asks.

"Yeah, we graduated together." And he once hurt and humiliated me, but I keep that tidbit to myself. "I thought he moved away. To Chicago or someplace." I try to sound very nonchalant, but I was happy when he left town right after high school, glad I'd never have to lay eyes on him again. Or so I thought.

"Indeed he did. Don't believe he's been back since. But Tom's in a bad way. He's with us at the manor now." By which she means Bluegrass Manor, the rehab and rest home where Helen puts her nursing skills to use.

That's another surprise. "I had no idea. What happened to him?" I don't know Tom Hutchins well, but he's become a fixture in our community, the guy you call when you need a deck or room addition built.

"At first they thought it was early onset dementia, but turns out the poor man has brain cancer. Wally took him for treatments, but it was too far gone." Wally Hutchins is Tom's brother, and the longtime owner of the building the red pickup sits parked in front of. "Wally and Edie had already put their house on the market and closed on their condo in Florida before Tom's diagnosis, so when the house sold, Tom insisted they go ahead with their move, not wanting to hold them up. But Wally called Travis in Chicago and told him he needed to get his butt down here and take care of family business—you know, look out for his dad and the farm and such, until Tom passes."

"Wow. That's a lot."

I'm still taking it in, in fact, when the truck's door finally opens and Travis Hutchins gets out. I'm dazed by the sight of him. Why couldn't he have gotten ugly over the past twelve years since graduation? Instead—ugh—he appears to have only become better looking. Once upon a time, he was a slightly rough, belligerent, long-haired kid in black clothes and combat boots. Now, his dark hair is much tidier and he looks like more of a rugged, flannel-and-denim-wearing guy.

"Morning," Helen calls to him as he walks toward the rear of the pickup.

Cringing inside, I instinctively make a move to head

back in the shop, but she grabs onto my wrist with catlike reflexes I've never noticed before.

Travis glances only briefly in our direction. "Morning." Okay, one thing hasn't changed about him—he still sounds a little belligerent. Like he'll be cordial if he must, but it pains him.

"Someone's up with the sun," she says cheerfully.

"Had to pick up a few things out at the farm." His voice is wooden—he's clearly being nice because he feels he has to, not because it comes naturally. So it throws me a little when he adds, "You're out early, too."

Helen points vaguely north. "I walk up to the bakery and get donuts for work when I have the morning shift." Then she motions to the east. "Guess I haven't mentioned that my house sits just around the corner on Grant Street. Will I see you at the manor today?"

He gives a short nod as he lowers the tailgate with a *clank*. "After I get some work done here."

"I don't know if you've heard," she says to me, loud enough that she's clearly trying to make this a group convo, "but Travis's Uncle Wally just sold the Lucas Building. While he's here, Travis is remodeling the ground floor for the new tenant and staying in the apartment upstairs."

Oh brother. I live in the apartment above *my* shop, too. And Travis Hutchins is *not* my idea of a good neighbor. "Ah," I say.

It's then that he looks up from whatever he's getting ready to unload from the truck and calls to Helen, "Anywhere I can get a cup of coffee this early?"

Fair question given that old Main Street, while somewhat lively during business hours, is mostly deserted otherwise. So I'm surprised yet again when she answers, "Sure—right here at the Christmas Box." She points over her shoulder at my shop.

"We're not really open yet," I remind her under my breath.

"Sure you are," she answers quietly.

"He can get coffee at the bakery," I reply through slightly-clenched teeth. Janie's Bakery is the only place in town *actually* open this early.

"Oh, that's all the way down the block," she says as if it's a trek through the Himalayas. "Your place is right here. You said you were excited to open, so open."

And just like that, she's off with a "Toodeloo," toddling her way toward the bakery—as Travis Hutchins abandons his unloading to cross the street toward me. "I'm not sure the coffee's ready yet," I tell him. Unfortunately, however, I did put a pot on before walking outside.

"I'm kinda desperate for it," he answers, "so I can wait."

And thus in a weird twist of fate, it would seem that Travis Hutchins, the boy who once stood me up on a very special night, is destined to be my very first customer at the Christmas Box.

As he follows me through the door, I feel fifty shades of awkward, not wanting to turn and find myself face-to-face with him.

"So this place is...what?" he asks.

"A Christmas shop," I answer shortly. I mean, does it not speak for itself? Trees dripping with tinsel and ornaments, stockings hung by the old chimney with care, colored lights, artificial snow, and Michael Buble crooning holiday standards over hidden speakers. What else *could* it be?

"Is it, like, a pop-up shop? Just open for a month?"

"No," I say, slightly annoyed. "We're open all year long." I've led him to the far end of the counter where the drink bar resides, and I check the coffee pot to find it's still dripping. Rats.

"And...you don't change it out to sell other stuff after Christmas?"

"Well, the name of the shop is the Christmas Box, so no." Again, is this a hard concept to grasp?

"Hmm," he says. It comes out sounding judgmental.

"Hmm?" I repeat to ask what he's hmming. I finally glance his way, sorry to discover he's just as handsome close-up as he was across the street.

Giving his head a short shake, he answers, "Nothing."

"Seems like *something*."

After a short hesitation, he says, "I'm just not a fan of Christmas, that's all. So it's hard for me to understand why anyone would want a never-ending holiday season. It's bad enough just getting through December. I wouldn't be able to handle all the fake warmth and fake cheer and fake snow all year long. I mean, don't take this the wrong way, but does *anyone* really want it to be Christmas all the time?"

I guess I *am* taking it the wrong way, because just who does this guy think he is? His attitude cuts to the very heart of my business model, a model that believes people want that Christmasy feeling for more than just the month of December. "First of all," I say, "the snow might be fake, but holiday warmth and cheer are very real. People *love* Christmas. They plan for it all year long. Christmas is about joy and giving and the holiday spirit—what's *not* to love? In case you haven't heard, it's the most wonderful time of the year."

He gives his head an argumentative tilt before shooting back at me, "Nope, the song got it wrong—it's the most *horrible* time of the year. Christmas is about commercialism, materialism, obligation, expectation, and being treated like you're letting the whole world down if you just want to live your life normally and not wear ugly Christmas sweaters all December long."

First, I take a deep breath—then I give him *my* point of view. "My family *treasured* Christmas. My dad died serving in Afghanistan when I was little, but my mom and grandma always made Christmas special for me, even when times were hard and my mother could have turned bitter. The two of them ran the Winterberry Diner that used to be next door, and they turned the place into a winter wonderland when the holidays rolled around. People loved their holiday spirit."

He squints, looking a little confused as he says, "I think I remember that place, but..."

"It's gone now," I confirm for him. "The whole structure. The park just outside, to the north of my building, took its place. I donated the lot to the town with the stipulation that it be made into a park named after my family."

He tilts his head. "Yeah, I noticed there was a building missing. What happened to it?"

"Mom and Grandma lived upstairs from the diner, and

The Christmas Box

there was a fire about ten years ago. I was away at college. They didn't get out."

I can see I've thrown him for a loop with my family tragedy. But he asked. "Sorry," he says. "That's awful."

I proceed onward to the point of my story. "Anyway, my mom always dreamed of opening a Christmas shop. She was saving toward it. So after she died, I started saving toward it. And then a few months ago, I quit my admin job working for the mayor, bought this building, and opened the shop. Or I'm about to in a couple of hours. Today is actually our first day."

His eyes get wider. And his deep voice softer. "Well, okay, I guess now I understand why you'd want a Christmas shop."

I, on the other hand, do not understand why he seemed so passionately Grinch-like about it. As someone whose livelihood now literally depends on people loving the holidays, I really want to know what his problem with Christmas is. "So why are you such a holiday hater?"

"I already told you." His reply is so short and blunt that I know there's more to the story.

But the coffee is done, so I grab a dark green, speckled mug with the words *Merry Christmas* and an old-fashioned Santa face stamped on the side and pour a cup, setting it on the counter in front of him.

And as he takes a sip, I realize I've made a terrible mistake. I should have put it in a paper to-go cup, and instead I've made it so he has to stay here to drink it. Rookie coffee bar mistake.

"You don't remember me, do you?" I hear myself ask,

unplanned. I'm not sure why; maybe because I'm tired of hearing him diss Christmas, an important aspect of my life, past, present, and—hopefully—future. Maybe because the longer we talk, the weirder it seems that it hasn't come up. Maybe because we're going to be neighbors, at least temporarily, and are we never going to acknowledge that we sat in the same homeroom for twelve entire school years?

As I look into his deep brown eyes and he looks back, I'm still trying to ignore how hot he is. He, on the other hand, is clearly trying to figure out the answer since I've put him on the spot. Finally he asks, "Were we in school together?"

"Yes." He's still puzzling it through, though, so I throw him a bone. "Think homeroom."

I should probably just tell him my name at this point—I hate when people I once knew make me play that terrible guessing game—but I suppose I'm still holding his Grinchiness against him.

That's when recognition dawns in his gaze. "Are you... Lexi? Lexi Hargrove?"

I raise my eyebrows—no smile—and say, "Bingo."

Then I watch his face fall as he remembers why this is relevant. I'm pleased it comes back to him instantly, pleased he's not going to pretend nothing bad ever happened between us. "We were supposed to..." He's wagging a finger back and forth between us now. "...Um, go to a thing together."

"Yes." I keep it short because maybe I suddenly regret reminding him of a time when he had the power to hurt

The Christmas Box

me. Funny how quickly those youthful feelings can come rushing back.

Now his face is a little scrunched up—and I realize he's still struggling to piece together the memory. "Why... didn't we?"

Well, I'm glad it made such an impact on him. He knows *something* went wrong between us, but he didn't bother to remember what. "You never showed."

He clenches his teeth and makes an "oops, ya got me" face. "That's what I was afraid of."

Maybe he's stood up a lot of girls in his day. Or maybe standing *me* up just wasn't a noteworthy entry on his list of high school sins. Either way, it adds insult to an old injury.

"I was kind of a punk back then," he goes on.

"Not a newsflash," I tell him. And if that was an apology, it's as weak as his memory.

"I'm not anymore," he claims.

I once again arch my eyebrows in his direction, this time to ask, "Are you sure?"

The question elicits a light laugh. It's the first time I've seen him smile, even if it fades quickly. "Well, I *try* not to be. Maybe I don't always get there. Got a lot on my mind lately."

"Helen told me about your dad. About why you're here."

"They say he doesn't have long."

"That must be hard." I don't really want to be nice to him, but a dying parent supersedes a lot, especially for me.

To my surprise, though, he just shrugs it off and resumes looking as sullen as he did getting out of his truck.

"We aren't close. Never have been. I'm here more for my uncle's sake than my dad's. As soon as he's in the ground, I'm gone, back to Chicago."

Whoa—what a cold thing to say. But then *I* remember something from high school that I'd totally forgotten until this moment. It seemed like he had a bad home life. His mother left when we were just kids, maybe fourteen or fifteen. And that's when he started the black-clothes-and-combat-boots things. I would have thought perhaps that kind of shared loss would make him closer with his father, but maybe not. And this is none of my business. So I change the subject. "I didn't know your uncle sold the building." His aunt and uncle ran a toy store in the old Lucas building for the last five years or so, until recently closing up shop.

"He and Aunt Edie are retiring down south." If I'm not mistaken, he's relieved by the change in topic. "But he put me in touch with the woman who bought it—she's opening a soap shop and hired me to build and install some custom shelving and cabinetry. That's what I do up in Chicago—along with other custom building."

"Like your dad," I say.

He blinks, looking oddly taken aback by the obvious. "Sort of, I guess."

Well, what started out as an awkward meeting has, unfortunately, stayed that way the entire time. I still wish he wasn't so nice to look at, with broad, flannel-covered shoulders, a day's dark stubble dusting a strong jawline, and those brown, brown eyes. Even though they're hard, his eyes, a reminder that he doesn't want to be here. In his hometown; at his dying father's bedside; in a Christmas shop. He seems like a very unhappy guy.

So I can't deny breathing a sigh of relief when he drains the last of the coffee from his mug and lowers it back to the old bar top with a *plunk* of finality. When he gets out his wallet and drops a bill next to the cup, I say, "I'll get your change."

"No need," he answers.

"It was a good cup of coffee."

"Well, okay. But only because I just remembered I don't actually have my cash drawer in place yet. We don't really open until nine."

"Then I appreciate you letting me in." And as he starts toward the door, he glances over his shoulder. "Good luck with your opening today." Then he slants me a grin. "But I still hate Christmas."

It's a nice grin. The kind it's hard not to grin back at. But I don't, instead suggesting, "Maybe you'll change your mind."

"Nope," he shuts me down quickly. "I'm here for one reason, a different kind of obligation than the ones that come with Christmas, and that's pretty much all I'm thinking about right now. So even if I get my coffee here, don't think you're gonna convert me into some kind of a Santaphile."

This *almost* makes me laugh, but I hold it in. And I'm tempted to tell him he can actually get early morning coffee up the street at the bakery—yet for some reason I don't.

As the sleighbells hanging on the door jingle behind his departure, I'm still wondering what happened with his family—to make his mother leave, to make his father someone he doesn't seem to care about, to make him hate Christmas so much. Reminded that we all have our losses, I suddenly feel a little more understanding about him being a punk back in school.

But the jury's still out on what he is now.

An hour and a half later, the sleighbells announce the next arrival and I look up to see Dara Burch, my friend and part-time employee. The fact that her long, black hair, streaked with strands of hot pink, is held back by a festive pair of fabric reindeer antlers, makes me smile. "Happy grand opening!" she greets me. "Are you excited?"

From behind the counter, I glance from side to side at all the stuff I've crammed into this shop. "Yes?" I don't intend it to come out like a question, but it's too late.

Her eyes widen with concern. "What's wrong? I mean, it's dream-come-true day. The lights are lit, the music is playing, every snowflake and gingerbread man is in place. Why do you look like a reindeer in headlights?"

The answer is something that's been weighing on me, but maybe I didn't let myself realize just how much until this morning. "What if we fail? What if the Christmas Box doesn't make it?"

I can see she gets it; she knows this isn't a sure thing. But that's when she points to a rustic painted wooden sign, currently hanging over the antique mantelpiece, which says: *Believe.* "You wouldn't have come this far if you didn't believe in the place."

"But what if I'm being naïve? What if I think we'll make it just because I want to honor my mom's wishes?"

"Look, every small business has to do what that sign says. And we have Christmas on our side—the *season* of believing."

"Of course. You're right." That's when I come back to myself, my usual self, the woman who looks at the world through hopeful eyes, despite everything, because that's what's gotten me through the dark times in my life.

Dara appears relieved. "Okay, that's better. There for a minute, I didn't even recognize you. But there's my glass-half-full friend, my 'everything will be okay' pal, my believer-in-miracles buddy."

"Opening day jitters," I tell her. "Because of course I believe. I believe in holiday magic, and I believe in the Christmas Box."

"Good—now we can get down to business. Want me to start the hot chocolate?"

"Go for it," I tell her, then reach beneath the bar for the Santa hat I've stashed there, pulling it onto my head. Glancing in a mirror, I flop the white, furry ball into just the right position.

"By the way, did you know there's a hottie working in the old toy store across the street?"

Yikes, did I ever. "That would be one Travis Hutchins."

From where she's measuring cocoa powder into the hot chocolate machine, she tilts her antlers. "Should I know him? Is he related to Wally and Tom?"

"No. And yes. He's Tom's son and he left Winterberry right after he high school—we graduated in the same class." I explain what I've learned about Tom's imminent passing and why his son has returned home.

"That's really sad," she says, now filling a water pitcher at an old sink we left installed near the bar. "But on the up side, he looks like he could make your Christmas merry."

I balk. "*My* Christmas? No thank you."

She's taken aback at my vehemence. "Sheesh—what did he ever do to *you*? Stand you up for a date in high school or something?"

I turn to face her. "Yes."

She flinches, her green gaze widening, the little diamond in her nose glittering beneath the lights. "I was kidding." She turns off the faucet just before the pitcher overflows.

"Well, I'm not. Though it wasn't *exactly* a date. But it was...an obligation on his part." As the word leaves me, I'm reminded how much he seems to resent obligations. "One that left me humiliated."

"Spill the tea, girl," she demands.

I let out a sigh at having to remember this twice in the same morning when I haven't thought about it in years. "In senior year, we were elected to represent our homeroom at the Winterberry Christmas Ball."

"Wow," she says. "I was *never* elected for anything like that."

"Neither was I, until then. I was just that quiet girl no one usually noticed," I explain since she was five years behind me in school, our friendship starting later. "So it came as a shock, and a nice one. It was a big deal to me. My grandma worked so hard making me a gorgeous emerald green gown."

"And then?"

"Well, you remember the tradition with the laurels."

She nods, looking a little resentful. "I wanted one of those things so bad." Despite the time between my graduation and hers, apparently the envy surrounding the laurels endured.

School tradition was that the guy went to the Holly Leaf Florist, just north of Winterberry in Holly Ridge, and ordered a custom head wreath, in Christmas colors, which he presented to the girl he was accompanying before the ceremony. The girls wore their wreaths as they were escorted across the gym floor, the bleachers filled with onlookers, and the one elected queen would place her wreath on the head of a favorite teacher before she was crowned. Cheesy, maybe, but every girl secretly wanted one of those pretty holiday laurels. And my time had finally come.

Except that it actually hadn't. "Well," I tell Dara, "I *still* never got one because Travis Hutchins stood me up. He just plain didn't come. I was the only girl walking by herself, and without a wreath."

"Ugh," Dara says. "That sucks."

"It was pretty humiliating," I go on. "Kids made fun of me, yelling across the gym, '*Guess he didn't want to be seen with you.*' '*Must've gotten a better offer.*'" I use my best fake nasty bully voice.

Looking back as an adult, it hardly mattered. But as an

insecure high-schooler who thought I was having a special night, it was devastating. "And get ready for the cherry on top. When Wendy Acara was elected queen, instead of giving her wreath to a teacher, she gave it to *me* instead." A lovely gesture from a popular girl who didn't have to be nice to me—but somehow it only seemed to shine a light on my embarrassment.

"Oh no," Dara says, her face etched with revulsion. "A pity laurel."

"Exactly. In front of the whole school."

And what made it worse was—maybe I developed a crush on him somewhere between the homeroom vote and the ball two months later. We barely spoke before, and we never spoke after—he never acknowledged not showing, and I never confronted him. But for a brief period of time, I suffered a niggling attraction that was, in the end, rewarded only with getting dissed.

I relocked the front door after he left earlier, and now, as opening time draws near, I head back up front. About to flip the lock again, I spot him working in the storefront across the street, surrounded by sawhorses, a big electric saw, and lots of wood. Done filling the cocoa machine, Dara steps up beside me. "A shame you have a bad history with him I love a man who's good with his hands."

"Then maybe I can fix *you* up with him the next time he comes in for coffee," I offer.

Her head darts around. "He came in for coffee?"

"Helen's fault. He asked where he could get some, and she sent him *here*. "

"The horror," Dara teases. "How dare she bring you business!"

"Well, he's not exactly who I wanted my first customer to be."

"Was he nice? Did he remember the Christmas dance that never was?"

I shrug. "He was a little surly. Mildly contrite at best. Didn't even seem to care that his father is dying. All in all, not my kinda guy."

Her shoulders slump slightly as we both turn to peer back across the street at the man operating the big saw. "Then not mine, either. But on a brighter note..." She casts me a sideways glance. "It's time to get this party started."

Indeed, cars are beginning to line the curb as Main Street comes to life. This morning wasn't what I expected, bringing doubts and unpleasant memories—but it's officially time to look forward. I flip the sign in the window that lets the world know the Christmas Box is open for business.

Travis

After a few hours of work in the soon-to-be soap shop, Main Street has gotten a little busy for my taste—people squinting to stare in as they walk past are making me feel like an animal in the zoo. I forgot how nosy small towns can be. So I take off my tool belt, wash some sawdust off at the bathroom sink, and head up the street to the new burger joint. Of course, I don't know *how* new it is, only that it's new to me. The old man asked me to bring him a big, greasy burger the next time I came—I guess when you're dying, they let you eat whatever you want.

The burger place is packed—in fact, *all* of Main Street is hopping in a way I never thought I'd see when I lit out of here at eighteen. The tables are filled, and servers are moving fast and carrying trays high as I step up to the counter. "Help ya?" asks an older lady with blonde hair piled on top of her head.

After I place my takeout order, I gravitate back to the wide front windows, mainly to get out of people's way while I wait.

Glancing out at the park across the street and a few doors down, I remember that the only business still open on Main when I left was The Winterberry Diner. It was bigger than most, taking up the space normally filled by two or three skinnier, pre-war buildings, as I remember my grandpa calling them. Seems ironic that the one staple of the place where I spent my whole life is gone now, but the rest of the town has been revitalized. In addition to the burger restaurant, there's a pizza place, an antique mall, a clothing boutique, and more. Not bad, Winterberry.

An awful shame about the diner—damn, it threw me when Lexi Hargrove so calmly told me her mom and grandma died there—but the park looks nice. I see some small trees and shrubbery, a manicured lawn with paved paths curving through, a few park benches, and to one side sits a white gazebo a lot like the one I built in my boss's backyard a few years ago. A big Christmas tree—currently unlit and probably twenty feet tall—stands in the center of the park.

That's when I take my first real look at the Christmas Box and begin to understand the shop's name. While most of the old brick facades are still in their original state, the two-story building just beyond the small park has been painted white, other than a strip of red that runs horizontally across the front and side. On the side, a vertical swath of red crosses it, with a big red bow painted where they intersect. Near the bow is a gift tag that reads *The Christmas Box*. She's turned the whole building into a Christmas gift. And granted, I'm not a Christmas guy, and I'm not sure how anybody's gonna feel about this place come June or July, but I can't deny it creates a pretty cool effect in this little old town.

Lexi Hargrove is the last person I expected to run into. I just would have thought she'd be somewhere else by now. Kind of sucks if she stayed just because of what her mom once dreamed of. I give my head a short shake thinking about people and their sentimentality when it comes to Christmas. It's just another day, after all—another day when people spend a lot of money on things they don't need.

She's prettier than I remembered—her wavy brown hair longer than when I knew her, and I never noticed how blue her eyes are.

Or maybe she was pretty then, too, but I just couldn't comprehend it. I was in a dark place, just getting through the days however I could. And now that I'm thinking back to high school, which I was happy to leave behind—I remember more about that dance.

I forgot to order the special head thing. And I didn't really have the money for it anyway. Every time it came to mind as the event got closer, I'd just shove it aside—it was something I just didn't want to do. It wasn't about her—I wasn't a kid comfortable parading around in front of the school in a suit I was gonna have to drum up someplace. I wasn't a jock, I wasn't a brain; I wasn't much of anything but angry. I should have turned the nomination down from the start, but it caught me off guard. The basketball player in our homeroom who usually got tapped for such events was absent that particular day and somehow my number came up.

And then I just didn't go. It would have been easy to tell somebody, make a phone call, at least claim I was sick or something. But I didn't even bother—instead I hung out with my small crowd of rebels at the Waffle House in Holly Ridge. I really *was* a punk back then.

"Order for Hutchins!"

I stride back to the counter, ready to scoop up my bag and go, but the lady holding it out—the same who took my order—asks, "You Tom's boy?"

I just nod. "Yep."

Her brow knits. "We're all real sorry about your daddy, son. Good you've come home to be with him. Tell him Gail Conrad and her family are all keepin' him in our prayers, and you, too—okay?"

Again, I only nod. "Thank you." Then I grab my bag and leave, my thoughts spinning in ten directions at once. Small town people are nosy, but they're also kind. Kind enough that she thinks *I'm* here out of kindness, or even love. And Helen, the nurse at Bluegrass Manor—and hell, all the people there, seem to think my dad's a great guy. I guess they have a short memory.

But I don't.

Walking into the nursing home feels like quietly immersing myself in a dark chaos. Every. Single. Time. I've been home less than a week, only come here on a handful of days, but it's a hard place to be. The people at Bluegrass Manor didn't have the money for a choice facility when the time came that they couldn't care for themselves anymore. So they ended up here, where the staff does their best, but it's not a setting where anyone would wish to spend their last days.

The first time I came, I felt tense, not having seen my old man in a dozen years. I wasn't sure if he'd treat it like a grand homecoming or spit on me. Turns out neither happened—instead, he just acted...completely casual. "Like he saw me yesterday," I told Helen later, confused.

Helen explained that, "In Tom's mind, maybe he did. Tom comes and goes in the past and present sometimes lately. Just roll with it and it'll all be okay." She patted my hand, and I tried to believe her, but as I walk through the sliding doors that lock behind me to keep the patients inside, I still feel like a stranger in a strange land.

The hallway is dotted by frail-looking people in wheelchairs. I see a thin-haired old woman I noticed yesterday— her short white hair points in all directions and she's cradling a bald, naked, plastic babydoll in her arms. The sight crushes my soul.

"Hey, can you help me? Please help me."

I swing my head around to look through the doorway the male voice came from.

"Can you help me?" he asks again, sounding desperate.

My impulse is to keep walking, but I've already made eye contact. So I step a little closer to the open door. "What do you need?"

He's old, feeble-looking, lying in a hospital bed in a stark, messy room. All the rooms are stark. He points. "Can you hand me the remote?"

It rests near a TV, and I'm instantly relieved this is all he's asking of me. I grab it up and hand it to him.

"And I need to go to the bathroom."

He's looking at me like I'm the guy for *this* job, too, but I say, "I'll let the nurses know."

Then I make a beeline down the hall, weaving between the wheelchairs and one spry lady using a walker, who says, "Hi, handsome," as I pass by.

"Hi," I say at a bit of a loss. That's my general feeling so far when under this roof—at a loss. I keep moving, pleased to see the nurse's station dead ahead.

"A guy up the hall needs help to the bathroom," I announce at large to Helen and two other nurses in the general vicinity.

Helen just laughs in her big, comfortable-with-the-world way. "Well, hello to you, too, Travis." Then, to a large, balding guy in scrubs with a goatee, she says, "Brent, wanna take this one?"

Brent turns toward me with gentler eyes than his stature led me to expect. "Which room?"

Great question. I didn't notice in my rush to get away. "About halfway down on the left. Guy in a robe." Then I roll my eyes at my own reply. *Most* of the guys here are wearing robes. I add, lamely, "I think it was plaid."

As Brent goes in search of Plaid Robe Guy, I ask Helen, "How is he today?"

She smiles. "Good. Looking forward to that burger—it's all I heard about this morning."

I nod and head to Dad's room, just a couple of doors away. But I stop and take a deep breath before going inside. That's just how it is—I have to brace myself, then push forward. Unlike that Christmas dance in high school, this time I can't just choose not to go.

"Got your burger and fries," I announce, holding the white paper bag high as I stride into the room.

Dad glances over, looking frail, but then he smiles. "I can smell it from here. Bring it on over."

I take a seat in the same old reclining chair he used at home when I was a kid—Wally brought it in, but I know from Helen that he's mostly in the bed and wheelchair now. As I unpack the bag on the rolling table like they have in hospital rooms, he asks, "Hope you got yourself one, too."

"I did," I inform him.

"Good—we can eat together." He points toward the mini-fridge at the foot of the bed, also courtesy of Wally. "Grab us a couple soft drinks, will ya?"

I brought in a twelve-pack yesterday, so I get two out. As he happily scarfs down a burger and fries while watching a rerun of a sitcom from before my time, all I can think is: This is not the father I remember. This must be the guy Gail at the burger place is praying for, and the man who brings a smile to Helen's face whenever I ask about him—but I don't know this guy.

The father I remember was always fighting with my mother, usually about money. The father I remember was often drunk—worst case scenario, he was screaming at me or Mom over nothing; best case, he sat passed out in the very chair in which I now reside, an empty beer can still clutched loosely in his fist. It The father I remember actually drank less but became more sullen and listless after my mother left us, making me feel mostly alone in the world. And the father I remember told me she'd left because of me.

I knew it wasn't true. It made no sense. I wasn't the one bitching at her all the time.

But it still stung, just the same. Especially when I was forced to acknowledge that she *did* leave me, too, not just him. She left her kid without even a goodbye. All of it *still* stings, if I'm honest with myself.

"Sure you don't want to stay for dinner?" Dad asks as I stand up to leave. "Your mom's making meatloaf tonight."

I flinch. Despite Helen's warnings, it's the first time I've heard him say something out of time.

"No, I gotta go," I answer. "Lot to do."

"Be back tomorrow? It's bingo day in the cafeteria."

And that fast, he's back in the present. I've seen the bingo game advertised on white boards around the manor. "Yep, I'll be back tomorrow," I tell him. But probably not for bingo. I'm challenged enough by my interactions *inside* this room, so I prefer to keep the ones outside it to a minimum.

I'm sheepishly glad Helen isn't at her station as I pass by, as if I think she's keeping tabs on me, maybe feeling I should stay longer. I've been here most of the afternoon, and that's enough. And I have shelves and cabinets to build. I'm grateful for the task, for other things to focus on. Actually, a lot of my job in Chicago has become more about management lately and less about actually constructing things, and just the few hours I got to work this morning made me realize I kinda miss it.

I turn the corner only to meet up with the thin-haired lady holding the babydoll. She peeks up at me with sad, childlike eyes. Our gazes connect and I wonder if she has the awareness to see the horror in mine.

"Have a nice day," I say, skirting past her. What do I even mean by that? They're just words spilling out of me, trying to fill a strange, painful void.

"Travis Hutchins, is that you?"

What now? I stop, look to my right. Through a doorway I see another man in another robe in another bed. But then I tilt my head as recognition comes. "Mr. West?"

"One and the same," he says.

Mr. West was my shop teacher in high school, the only teacher who ever made me feel like I mattered. Maybe the fact that it was the only class in which I applied myself was a factor there, but I was in full punk mode by then, so I have to credit him with looking beyond what I was putting out in the world at that time. Other than graying hair and a few more creases in his face, he hasn't changed much.

As I step into his room, he says, "Sorry about your father."

"Sorry to see *you* in here," I tell him with unguarded honesty.

"Oh, I'll be sprung soon enough," he informs me. "Just some rehab after knee surgery. Another week and I'll be home in my own bed."

"I'm sure that's a relief," I say before thinking it through. Then I shake my head and say, "I just mean..."

He nods, absolving me. "It's a tough place," he acknowledges. "Lot of people in bad situations."

You can say that again.

"You still teaching?" I ask.

"No, retired last year and living the good life," he tells me. "Well, once I get back mobile again, that is. The wife and I bought an RV and we're gonna travel the country. What about you? Doing well? Think I heard you were in Chicago."

I nod. "I've been working for a custom home builder the last ten years. I've made a good career out of woodworking and construction," I tell him. "In no small thanks to you."

Mr. West just shrugs and gives a low chuckle. "You already knew what you were doing by the time you landed in my class. Your dad had already taught you more than I ever could."

I take that in, letting it remind me of something Lexi Hargrove said this morning. I guess I *did* spend a lot of time out in Dad's workshop with him as a kid. Not so much later, when the drinking started, and certainly not after Mom left—but even if I don't like to admit it, I suppose the guy did give me some skills.

"So, got a girlfriend?" Mr. West asks. "Married? Kids?"

I just laugh. "None of the above."

"Well, maybe soon then," he suggests.

But I feel the urge to be honest, something I was always able to do with him. "Not likely," I say. "I mean, girlfriends, yeah. But not sure I'm cut out for anything permanent. Lack of role models, ya know?"

His nod tells me he remembers. Sometimes I stayed late after class, the last period of the day, and we'd talk. "Are things better between you and your dad now?"

But I barely know how to answer. "Truth is, until a few days ago, I hadn't seen him since high school."

My old confidante's eyes bolt open wide.

"I left for Chicago right after graduation and never looked back. For the first few years he would call me up from time to time—on my birthday or Christmas. But it was awkward and he eventually stopped. I kept in slightly closer touch with my Uncle Wally, so Dad and I each knew the other wasn't dead or anything—but that was it until Wally insisted I take a leave of absence from my job and come home."

Compassion fills my old teacher's gaze. "How has it been since you got here?"

I shrug. "Weird. I don't even recognize him. Apparently brain cancer has made him a much friendlier guy than the one I grew up living with. But...fine, I guess. And I'll stay until he goes. Just a matter of waiting, and then I can get back to my real life."

At this, Mr. West tilts his head. "Don't you want to talk things through with him while you still can?"

I take a moment, turning the idea over in my brain, and finally tell him, "Even if I did, I'm not sure he'd be able to. He just told me my mother was making meatloaf for dinner."

Mr. West gives a solemn nod of understanding—yet then he adds, "It's none of my business, Travis, but be that as it may...just think about clearing the air. If not for him, then for you. I wouldn't want you to have any regrets about that after it's too late."

"I'll think about it," I answer. But I'm lying. Just to be respectful to someone who's earned that from me. If anybody should have cleared the air, it's my old man, and it should have happened long before now.

December 1

Lexi

Nothing says the Christmas season is truly upon us like a good tree-lighting ceremony, and it was me who first suggested we start having the Annual Winterberry Tree-Lighting after the Hargrove-Munson Memorial Park was completed. The truth is, I donated the land for the park largely because the exorbitant cost to clear a lot that wasn't worth much at the time made it the only sensible move. But even now that Main Street is bustling, I'm not sorry, because it's a nice place and a fitting way to honor my family.

And this year's tree-lighting is extra-exciting for me. As I stand near the big evergreen we've all been decorating for weeks, Dara is next to me, along with her mom, who she's pushed here in a wheelchair from their small house a couple of blocks away. Helen, stationed across the park with some other Winterberrians, sends me a mittened wave.

"Ready?" Dara asks.

I nod—then find myself scanning all the friends and townspeople circled around the tree, all of us in our winter parkas and hats and gloves. Despite myself, I fear maybe I'm looking for...him. Travis Hutchins. God only knows why—because as I'd hoped, I haven't run into him again.

He's been in for coffee twice in the past week since our grand opening, but I was helping a customer in another part of the shop both times and Dara rung him out. Her assessment was, "As hot as I thought, but you're right—kinda grouchy."

It's stayed on my mind, him being such a holiday hater. Maybe I just think it's sad. Hating Christmas, plus having a dad who's dying and clearly being emotionally blocked off about that—yikes.

"Hey there—how's business at your new place?"

I look up to see the much-more-pleasant Jordan Costa from Thoroughbred Pizza, one of our popular Main Street spots, at my side.

"So far, so good," I tell the hardworking, thirty-something guy who brought Italian food to Winterberry. The truth is, we've been busy and I already love my new life as a shopkeeper—but the further truth is, just yesterday Chet Wheeler gave me a number I need to reach by December 25, and I'm...concerned. If we keep up the current pace, I'll make it, but just barely, so it's enough to have me on edge. "Please send people my way."

"You know I will, Lex."

That's when my old boss, Mayor Gary Witlow, steps up to the microphone in the nearby gazebo. "Welcome to the Seventh Annual Winterberry Tree-Lighting Ceremony."

The crowd applauds and I can't deny loving my little community. I could have left after my family was gone, but Hargroves and Munsons have populated Winterberry for over a century, and every time I thought about leaving, it felt like I would surely be losing more than I could ever gain. I just hope the Christmas Box thrives the same way the Winterberry Diner always did.

"After the lighting," Gary continues, "we'll sing some carols and drink some cocoa, but first, we'll carry out one of my favorite Winterberry traditions, in which the proprietor of our newest Main Street business places the star on top. It's altogether fitting that this year the honor goes to our own Alexandra Hargrove, a young woman I personally know very well. I've had the pleasure of working with Lexi since she graduated from the University of Kentucky until just recently, when, sadly for me, she tendered her resignation in order to follow her dream of opening a shop here on Main Street. She's a hometown girl—and for anyone who doesn't already know, she generously donated the land for this very park. Her family was the pride of Winterberry, and I'm sure they're smiling down on us tonight, ready to watch as Lexi puts our star atop the tree. Step on up here, Lexi."

The ladder has wide steps and I've been given a long stick-like gadget that will allow me to place the star. I've practiced using it on lower trees several times, but the pressure is really on now.

The mayor is still waxing poetic as I carefully begin to climb, and though I'm concentrating on the task at hand, I'm also aware that it's just started snowing a little.

"Look!" I hear a little girl cry out. "Snow, Mommy! Snow!"

Only flurries, but the timing still seems perfect and a little magical.

As I rise higher, star stick in hand, I catch sight of a silhouetted figure in the window of the Lucas Building across the street. Travis Hutchins. He didn't bother walking twenty steps to our community gathering, but he's standing inside, backlit, unaware I see him watching.

My mother and grandmother taught me that when you put a star on top of a tree, you make a wish—a wish upon a star. And I always have. lot lately, in fact—getting the trees in the shop decorated before we opened had me wishing right and left. I've wished for happy lives—for me, for Dara, for Helen, for good health for friends and neighbors, for a thriving Winterberry, for lots of other things. And as I reach the top of the Winterberry town tree and extend the sparkling star toward the top bough, I send up one more: I wish for Travis Hutchins to find the joy of Christmas.

The wish enters my head quickly, with no time to rescind or even fine-tune it, as I slowly lower the star onto the top of the tree with careful precision. And when I gently release it, it stays—hallelujah!

While the crowd below me cheers and applauds, someone calling, "Good job, Lexi," it hits me that I've come a long way in this town since being the girl who was embarrassed to walk across the gym floor alone.

And as for that wish for someone I don't even like... well, guess I'm just a nice person. Or maybe I think finding Christmas joy might make *him* a better person. So I've officially done my good deed for Travis Hutchins.

Once I'm back on the ground, the mayor starts a countdown. "Ten, nine, eight, seven..." I keep my eye on the star, thinking of the man across the street who, frankly, *seems* like he needs someone to send up some wishes for him. Maybe that's why I did it. A pity wish. Sort of like a pity laurel.

"...Three, two, one. Light it up!"

The tree illuminates with thousands of colored lights that make us all ooh and ahh.

And me, I'm thinking about wishing. Wishing is magic. Wishing is hope. I'm still not sure why I care, but I hope my wish tonight comes true.

Travis

The tree is pretty, I'll admit that much. But when I look at all those people getting so excited about it, I remember why I'm better off living someplace where things move a little faster, where more happens, where people aren't so damned sentimental.

Oh God, now they're singing Christmas carols. I feel like I've just shown up in Whoville on Christmas morning—next thing you know, they'll break out the roast beast. But my heart hasn't grown three sizes, or even one. Life's not a cartoon.

My strange existence here has fallen into a sort of routine. My time is split between getting the old Lucas building ready for its new life as a soap shop and spending more time at the nursing home. Dad is still eating burgers like they're going out of style and acting like a man I never knew. I've learned the lady with the babydoll is named Dottie, and I've also gotten acquainted with a number of the other "residents," as the nursing staff respectfully calls them. Not how I saw my life at thirty playing out, but I'm used to the universe throwing me curveballs—so this is just one more. And I won't be stuck here forever.

Mr. West checked out a couple of days ago. Good for him, though I'll miss seeing him when I'm there.

I'd planned to start clearing out the old farmhouse by now. After Dad's gone, it'll be mine, so I need to get it ready to put on the market. But so far I've only been there once—the morning I ran into Helen and Lexi on the street—to check on the place and get some winter clothes Dad wanted from his closet. I'd woken up early, unable to sleep, and went before the sun even came up. It was weird being there, and I just haven't felt like going back.

As the crowd across the street begins to disperse, I find myself watching, trying to pick out familiar faces. But it's dark, the night air illuminated by only the Christmas lights in the park and on the buildings, along with a few streetlamps.

I know who I'm looking for, though, and even with the lack of light, it's not hard to narrow in on Lexi Hargrove when she approaches the front door of her shop, unlocking it to go inside. Despite myself, I've stayed intrigued by a woman who's suffered such huge losses and still bounces around being all merry and bright. Has she somehow deluded herself? Or does she know some secret to life I don't?

Turning out the last of the lights in the soap-shop-in-progress, I head up the back stairs, grab a frozen dinner from the freezer to pop in the microwave, then reach for the remote and turn on the TV. *Please let there be something on besides Christmas shows.*

December 2

Lexi

Dara is ringing out customers, today's antler headgear accented by a Rudolph hoodie, while I start a new batch of hot chocolate and put on a fresh pot of coffee. We've just had a nice little afternoon rush, and it's those rushes that help me believe the Christmas Box will survive to see a second holiday season next December. *Please, please, please,* I whisper inside—to God or whoever else might have a hand in such things.

When I hear the door sleighbells jingle just after four, I glance up to see my cousin Haley and her two adorable toddlers. My mom and her dad were siblings. I saw them just over Thanksgiving at her parents' house up north in the Cincinnati suburbs, and I invited the whole extended family to visit the shop anytime, but given how busy people are this time of year, I didn't expect anyone to actually take me up on it.

"Haley!" I wave from the end of the bar, then rush to meet her and the kids, currently in a double stroller that she's just wrangled through the door.

"Lex, this place!" she exclaims. "It's everything you said and more. Christmas heaven!"

I look around at my own personal holiday wonderland, pleased with her reaction. "It *is* pretty dreamy, isn't it?"

She nods, wide-eyed, then drops a glance to the little ones. "I'm just sorry these two have already conked out. I thought they'd love it. On the other hand, this way I don't have to worry about tiny hands grabbing at breakable things, and I can actually just, you know, *shop*. I've almost forgotten what that feels like."

I nod—as if I know. The truth is, I secretly envy my cousin's lovely little family, along with her wonderful marriage to her architect husband, Ben. Haley and I are near the same age and loved playing together growing up. We would daydream about the future, and I recall her wishing for a glamorous career in fashion design. Instead, she runs a bakery with her sister, Hannah, has a beautiful home, a handsome husband, and these adorable kids. In short, I sometimes feel like Haley got all of *my* dreams—a small, thriving business and a loving family to come home to at night. But I finally have my shop, and as for the rest, I accepted long ago that not everyone gets the perfect happy ending, and that it doesn't all have to *be* perfect to be happy.

That's when I shift my gaze out the front window,

catching sight of enormous snowflakes against the backdrop of a certain red pickup across the street. "Looks like it's starting to snow."

Haley turns to see. "Oh, wow, yeah. We had some flurries last night, but this seems like more, doesn't it? I'd better get shopping in case it keeps coming down and has me racing for home." It's a forty-five minute drive in *good* weather, so I get it.

"If you want to leave the stroller with me, we're quiet right now."

Her eyes light up. "Are you sure?"

"Absolutely."

Half an hour later, neither child has cracked an eyelid, and Haley has bought several gifts, along with new ornaments for her tree and a cute advent calendar for the wall. The snow has continued to fall, so I make sure the presents for the kids are hidden deep within shopping bags, then help her get everything to her SUV, parked just outside the door.

Cars and awnings are already covered with a layer of snow, and though the streets are only wet, the sidewalk is starting to pick up a thin coating of white, as well.

"Crazy to get such heavy snow this early," Haley says as we buckle the babies into their car seats.

I nod. It's not unheard of, but not normal, either. "I didn't see a thing about this in the forecast."

As she gets behind the wheel and we say our goodbyes, I tell her to drive carefully and text me when she gets home. By the time I'm back inside, the last shopper is headed out and the store is suddenly still and quiet other than Taylor

Swift singing about a Christmas tree farm through the overhead speakers.

And I'm suddenly overcome with an inexplicable sadness.

I can't put my finger on why—maybe it's a lot of things.

I can't call it loneliness—Dara is here, after all, straightening gift bags hanging on the wall. And we've had plenty of foot traffic today—this is the first time there hasn't been at least one or two customers in the shop.

Maybe it's the unanticipated snow—something I'd normally love this time of year. But Main Street emptied almost entirely in just the short time it took to get Haley on her way. Suddenly, a snowfall I would otherwise find enchanting becomes an enemy—to my business and *every* small business trying to stay afloat on Main.

But it's only one afternoon. And maybe it'll stop anytime now.

I tug my phone from my pocket and pull up a weather app. After which my jaw drops before I announce to Dara, "So the forecast has changed. They're suddenly calling for three inches before it stops tonight around eight."

"Oh, crud," she replies. "I was planning to get groceries after work—I've pretty much let us run out of food."

"You should go *now*," I tell her without a second's hesitation. Being caregiver for her mother is Dara's top priority. Her older siblings provide financial support and she provides the care—her work with me is mostly to give her a break and get her out of the house.

"Are you sure? What if it gets busy again?"

With another glance out the window, where the only

movement is the snow descending in thick, heavy flakes, I say, "I don't think it will. In fact, I have a feeling we're done for the day. You go on. I'm fine here."

She nods. "You're probably right." Shedding her antlers, she bundles up in a tie-dye parka, pulls on a hot pink winter hat, then sets out up the snow-covered sidewalk.

Of course, that leaves the shop even quieter. Sure, holiday music continues to play, but something about it almost depresses me—because who is it playing for, after all?

I glance around, taking it all in, and yes, it's a winter wonderland, and yes, business is good—but...is something missing?

Maybe this is the first time since we opened that I've had the chance to stand here alone and take in the Christmas Box, *without* the customers, *without* Dara, *without* rushing to restock shelves or wash coffee cups.

And I'm slightly horrified to look around at the sparkling trees, twinkling lights, Santa mugs, and smiling snowmen and realize: it's just a shop.

Somehow, I wanted this to be *more* than just a small town store, *more* than just a tribute to my mother, *more* than just a way to make a living doing what I feel passionate about. I wanted it to feel truly *magical*. I wanted it to spread the love of Christmas I shared with Mom and Grandma. I wanted it to hold charm and warmth and a feeling that all is right in the world.

A tall order, I know. And perhaps an unrealistic expectation. But also a thing I thought would just natu-

The Christmas Box

rally, organically happen when I put all the pieces together.

I wanted people to walk through the door and feel the same way *I* felt last night placing that star on top of the tree and making that wish for the Grinchy hottie across the street: Filled with hope. Filled with possibility. Filled with belief.

And instead…it's just a shop.

And maybe it's silly to have expected it to be anything more than that. Christmas is in the heart, after all—not hanging on the branches of an evergreen or tucked into a glittery gift bag.

And yet, even so, what if there *was* a way to make people who come to the Christmas Box feel the same as I did putting that star on the tree? What if there was a way to fill every person who walked through the door with that same sense of hope and anticipation? What would that look like?

A box. I don't know where the words come from. It's almost like they're whispered in my ear. But I know instantly what they mean.

The next question is: Where do I get the perfect box? Because it can't be just *any* box. It has to be unique and special—a box that gives off the same sense of magic I want to create with it.

I'm kind of excited as I start thinking about it—my heart begins to race. But *where, where, where* do I find this perfect box?

I let my eyes drift from floor to ceiling, from back wall to front windows, as if the answer lies hidden somewhere inside the store. Which is when my gaze falls on the shiny red pickup across the street, now covered in a layer of snow. It's the only vehicle still left outside, and lo and behold, Scrooge McHottie himself has just come outside to get something from the truck bed.

What bizarre impulse compels me to rush out and across the empty street without even first grabbing a coat? I'm not completely sure, but...he builds things. And time is short. And he's right in front of me. So it makes sense, right?

I approach as he hoists slats of wood up onto his shoulder to carry inside, noticing he *was* smart enough to put on a coat.

"Could you build me a wishing box?"

He squints at me through the snow like I have reindeer antlers sprouting from my head—and not the fake kind. "A whatting box?"

"A wishing box."

"Can you close the tailgate?" he asks, occupied with balancing the wood.

I slam it shut, then follow him to the Lucas Building, holding the door for him.

"It should be about this big," I go on once we're inside, holding my hands about eighteen inches apart, "and have a unique style that looks a little magical and like maybe it came straight out of Santa's workshop. It should make people ooh and ahh when they see it—the very sight should draw them closer. Can you do that?"

He plunks the bundle of wood in his arms onto the old counter at the rear of the space and turns to face me. "So you're saying you want me to make you a magic box." He's still squinting, as if checking to make sure he hasn't misunderstood.

"Well, it doesn't really have to *be* magic," I explain. "It just needs to *look* magic."

"A magic-*looking* box," he repeats. Then murmurs sarcastically, "Sure, nothing odd about that."

"I figure if you can make pretty cabinetry out of wood, you can make a pretty box, too, right?"

He shrugs, now appearing a smidge smug. "Well, right." Then he gives his head a pointed tilt. "And you need this magic-looking box for...?"

"For the shop," I say. "For the wishes." I'm speaking excitedly, wanting him to get this and unsure why he doesn't.

But now he's shaking his head. "What wishes? What are you talking about, woman?"

"I told you, it's a wishing box. For people to put their Christmas wishes in."

He's still looking at me like I'm crazy.

And I can't make it any simpler, so I move on. "I'll pay you whatever you want. Price is no object." Though then I backtrack. This is what comes of rushing ahead with an idea before thinking it through. "Within reason, I mean. I *am* trying to get a small business off the ground here, after all."

He lets out a laugh. And ugh, it makes him so much more attractive when he's not scowling or acting all serious and grim. "Look," he says, "I can make you a box, no charge. Or...coffee on the house maybe?"

"That's great," I tell him. "Coffee for life." Though,

again, perhaps I should think more carefully before blurting things out from sheer enthusiasm.

Now, though, his brow knits again. "Just...explain to me a little more what the purpose is. Wishing?"

I nod. "It needs a slot on the top where you can slide a slip of paper in. Christmas is a time for wishing, and if people can come into the Christmas Box and make a wish, it will give them the sense that miracles can happen if you just believe. You know?"

He pushes out a long sigh, eyeing me through a narrowed gaze. "What I know is...you're a little loopy when it comes to all the Christmas stuff— but like I said, I'll make your box. And I'll be collecting on that coffee arrangement." He ends with a wink that A) I didn't expect, and B) makes me feel a little fluttery inside.

"Deal," I say, holding out my hand for a handshake.

He takes it, his touch shockingly warm given that we've both just been out in the cold. "Deal." And that makes me even *more* fluttery. I cringe inside at my own response.

Though quick as that, the touching is over, and now he's moved on to looking puzzled about something else. "Was it supposed to snow?"

I shake my head. "But now they say it'll keep coming down until well after dark."

He offers a slight grimace in reply. "Maybe I should start over to the manor before it gets any deeper out there."

I'm secretly amused that he's already referring to the nursing home as "the manor," same as the locals. "Is it safe in your truck?" I ask. "My grandpa had a '56 Ford when I was little and it was no good in the snow."

"Mine'll plow through anything," he claims, and I think it's just masculine bravado at first, until he goes on—maybe because I look skeptical. "It belonged to my great-grandfather and got passed down. My dad gave it to me when I turned sixteen. Since then, I've overhauled it from top to bottom. Automobile purists don't like it, but I wanted to drive the thing—not leave it sitting in a garage. I outfitted it to be reliable in the snow, for Chicago winters."

"Well then," I say, "sounds like I don't have to worry about you making it there alive."

He tilts me a sly half-grin I didn't see coming. "You would worry about me? And here I didn't think you liked me much."

I just roll my eyes. "We just made a deal for a box. I want to be sure I get it." Then I find myself flashing a slightly combative look. "Though I hope you'll do better getting me the box than you did that Christmas laurel back in school."

"Touché," he answers with an arch of one brow. "And just FYI, I'm a lot more reliable these days."

"Fingers crossed that's true," I tell him, holding up two intertwined fingers, still not fully convinced. Then I start toward the front door.

"Think Winterburger stayed open through this?" he asks behind me.

I stop, look back, then hold my hand out level, tipping it back and forth. "Iffy."

"Dad loves their burgers. Can't get enough of 'em."

Maybe this is nosy, but since he was honest with me about this before, I decide to ask. "Are things...better than you expected? Between you and him?" I almost add that it seems like he spends a lot of time at Bluegrass Manor, but I don't want to let on that I notice his comings and goings.

He releases a tired-sounding sigh to answer, "They're... okay. I barely recognize the guy, actually. But being a nice guy *now* doesn't make up for being a shitty dad *then*."

I just nod. I could argue the point, but I don't know if I'd be right. I had loving parents, so I haven't walked in his shoes.

Together, we head toward the shop's front door and both glance down at the same time to see a couple of dark eyes peering back through the glass. I quickly realize they're attached to a scruffy white dog who almost blends into the backdrop of snow. He looks like a cross between a Jack Russell terrier and...something else, so kind of a mutt. But a pretty cute one.

"Somebody lose their dog?" Travis asks, looking annoyed. Doesn't take much to annoy this guy, and I'm actually pretty stunned he agreed to make the box, even if he *did* act like it was weird.

"I don't recognize it," I tell him. "And no collar—might be a stray."

"Rough weather to be lost in." The words sound more like observation than compassion, though.

"At least the overhang might keep him dry if he stays here until the snow stops." The building's entryway is recessed, with an antique mosaic penny tile design between the door and the sidewalk. Even without a star to put on a tree, I send up a silent wish for the dog to be kept warm and safe. Season of miracles, after all.

We both ease out the door in a way that keeps the poor dog from getting in. Then, as the three of us stand there on the old tile, snow still falling an arm's length away, Travis asks, "You think if I let him in here while I'm gone, he'd go to the bathroom on the floor?"

Of course I think he would, but given the weather, I hear myself tell a tiny white lie. "Maybe he'll be so grateful that he'll just curl up and go to sleep."

Travis looks as doubtful about this as I feel, but he reopens the plate-glass door and shoos the dog inside. "It's your lucky night," he calls behind it as it goes rushing in. "Don't poop on my stuff!"

After he locks the door, he glances back at me to notice, "You're not wearing a coat." Like with the dog, it's more observation than concern.

"When I got the idea about the box and saw you outside," I explain, "I got excited and rushed over to ask you."

At this, another teasing, half grin makes its way onto his handsome face. "I think you and I have different ideas about what's exciting. You'd better get inside before you freeze to death."

"And you'd better get to Winterburger before they shut down for the day." A glance up the street reveals their lights are still on.

As we both start in different directions in the snow, he calls, "You have a nice night, Lexi Hargrove."

I already suspect the night I'm going to have, however, will be filled with the questions already dancing like sugar plums in my head: Will I really get that box? Will it somehow be the missing ingredient in my recipe for holiday magic at the Christmas Box? And...did Travis Hutchins' just flirt with me? Then again, calling me loopy isn't exactly a wooing move, so maybe I misread some of that.

And the most troubling question: Why did I get all fluttery at the mere touch of his hand? Yes, I would like for him to find holiday joy—but that does *not* mean I want mystery flutterings from the guy. Those are two different things entirely, and one of them is *not* on my Christmas menu.

December 3

Travis

No matter how much time I spend at the manor, leaving always feels like an escape. Partly because I still don't know this man who's never acknowledged his poor parenting or the fact that I got out from under his roof the second I turned eighteen and never came back. So after having a quick lunch with Dad, as I move past the nurse's station, waving to Helen and a younger redheaded nurse named Gabbi, I suffer a familiar eagerness to reach the door and burst back out into the sunlight.

That's when a hand closes over my wrist, halting me in place. I look down to see a woman in her forties with dark, shoulder-length hair and glasses, in a wheelchair. She's wearing fleece pants sporting images of Olaf from Frozen. She says something, but I can't understand her slurred speech. It makes me feel bad, and on edge, to have to ask, "Can you repeat that?"

She does, but I have no idea what she's saying. I feel even worse now. I must be looking at her like a lost puppy. And she's looking at *me* with exasperation in her eyes.

Undaunted, however, she tugs at my arm as she maneuvers the wheelchair through a doorway into what I'm guessing is her room. As much as I'd rather not go in, I'm not mean enough to pull away. The room is tidier than many, and blatantly girlish with a pink flowered comforter on the bed topped by a lavender-and-white-yarn afghan. Small plush animals, only three or four inches tall, line the back of a small, wooden writing desk. Above the bed on the wall hang pink-and-purple wooden letters from a craft store that spell out *Shannon*.

She's still talking to me in words I don't understand, and now I'm forced to tell her, "I'm sorry—I just don't know what you're saying."

She rolls her eyes, like I'm an imbecile. Maybe I am. Then she wheels herself over to a chest of drawers in front of the room's one window, points to it, mimics pushing it, and then gestures to a spot about five feet away.

"Ohhhh," I say, at last understanding. "You want me to move the chest for you."

Her eyes grow wide as she nods profusely. I can almost hear her thoughts: *Finally, you get it, dummy*.

I have no idea what's so urgent about this, but maybe if you're stuck in here and you see a guy who looks like he can move the piece of furniture you need moved, you don't let him get away. There were times I felt helpless as a kid, but this has me thinking about helplessness in a whole different way. It's not the first time a resident here has boldly insisted I help them in some way. I guess they don't have the luxury of being subtle or polite.

So I shove the chest until she seems happy with where it is. And although it's muffled-sounding to me, I *am* able to make out the words when she says, "Thank you."

Then, as if I'm not still standing there, she rolls her chair over to the window, angling it just so, and peers out. I glance out, too. Cardinals flit around in the snow, looking like a living Christmas card. Now I get it. She wanted to sit by the window, but the chest was in the way. I've never wanted to sit by a window that badly. But then again, I've never not been able to.

Pretty sure she's done with me, I lift an awkward wave and say, "Enjoy the birds," and exit back into the hallway with its usual cluttered array of wheelchairs and walkers.

"I see you met Shannon."

I spin to find Helen approaching behind me, wearing the same inviting smile as usual.

"Yeah, I moved a chest of drawers for her. I felt bad, though," I admit. "I couldn't understand her when she spoke."

Helen just pleasantly head-shakes it away. "She's used to it. She had a stroke."

After seeing how it left someone who probably thought she was in her prime, I wince at the word. "She seems young for that."

Helen shrugs, walking alongside me now. "It happens. She's a sweet soul. Lonely. Her family doesn't visit much."

"That sucks."

Helen just nods. "It's that way for a lot of the residents. They get forgotten. Left behind." She reaches down to give my hand a quick squeeze. "That's why it's so good that you're here for your dad. I know it's disrupting your life right now. But you're a good son."

Such a gross inaccuracy makes me draw back slightly—accepting wrongful praise doesn't feel right. "I only came because Wally asked me to. In fact, he pretty much insisted. So I'm not that great of a son—trust me."

But she still seems set on letting my inadequacies slide. "You're here. Pretty much every day. If you're not a good son, you're faking it well."

We're nearing the front door now, so rather than argue the point, I just say, "See you tomorrow, Helen."

"You probably don't realize this," she goes on, "but for many people here, I'm the last face they see, the one holding their hand as they die. It's heartbreaking."

Everything here is heartbreaking. But I don't tell her that. She and the rest of the staff do everything they can for the people in their care.

"That's why it matters," she continues as I stop to look back at her. "That you're here. One less person has to pass from this world feeling alone."

As I cross the snowy parking lot to my truck, I know I'm still faking it, just like she said. And I can't help thinking my dad is doing a good job of faking the good-father routine, too. No one knows the details of our history other than Mom walking out on us, so even people here at the manor who see him smiling and being nice—they don't understand what my teen years were like. Helen might think I'm a good son, but I'm just going through the motions—until I'm done and can leave for a second time, never to darken this town's doorstep again.

Next up on my agenda today: a trip out to the farm. I've promised Lexi Hargrove a "magical" wooden box, and my dad's old workshop will likely have everything I need. I could've constructed it in the storefront where I'm working —but I didn't bring my hand-carving tools, so I can use Dad's.

The narrow road leading to where I grew up hasn't been cleared of snow yet, but the truck takes every curve with ease. When I pull up outside the modest white farmhouse, I study it from the gravel drive. It could use a coat of paint, but otherwise looks about the same as I remember. On the far side of the front yard stands a large apple tree that never produced fruit—but a tire swing the old man put up when I was little still hangs from a thick rope I can't believe hasn't rotted away. Vague memories of him pushing that tire, me holding on tight and laughing as it swung in the summer breeze, flash briefly in my head.

I should check on the house again. My grandfather once told me a house that isn't lived in falls into disrepair quicker. "Almost like it knows it's being neglected," he said. I haven't been here for a week, so I pull a keychain from my pocket—one that's gotten heavier lately with Dad's keys— and unlock the front door.

It smells musty, so despite the furnace bill, I open a couple of windows, figuring it's just for a few minutes. I walk around checking things out. Familiar curtains, now faded, hang in the windows of my youth. I turn on faucets and flush toilets, just to keep them all doing what they're supposed to do. Eyeing the old washer and dryer, tucked into a tiny room off the kitchen, it occurs to me I could bring my laundry here rather than search out a laundromat. I have a moment of missing the modern laundry room in my Chicago townhouse—luxurious in comparison to everything here—but maybe it's good to be reminded where I come from and how far I've gotten.

That's when I head toward a room I didn't enter in my quick in-and-out last week—my boyhood bedroom. I wonder what the old man's done with the place.

And when I walk through the doorway, I couldn't be more stunned to see…it's exactly as I left it. Same blue patchwork quilt on the bed, made by my grandmother. Same red beanbag chair. Same posters on the wall of Katy Perry and Jennifer Lawrence.

It's a little too blast-from-the-past for me, though. Too much like I just stepped back in time. My chest tightens slightly.

Who was I then? An angry kid with every reason to be angry. A scared kid, who knew I needed to get out of here, but had no idea where I was going. A hurt kid, whose mother abandoned him and whose father neglected him. I leave the room, giving my head a brisk shake to clear out those old cobwebs.

Making my way back to the living room to close the windows and shut out the wintry air now pouring in, I'm still caught off guard that he never changed it. Was he just too lazy? Or…did he think I was coming back someday?

I'm about to lock the place back up and head out to the workshop when my eyes fall on a framed picture next to the spot where his recliner used to sit facing the TV. It's of...me. I was about ten. I'm smiling wide—not cool enough to scowl at cameras yet—and holding up a big largemouth bass I caught fishing with Dad at Winterberry Lake. I'd forgotten about that day. Maybe I've forgotten about actual *good* days when I was a kid, too traumatized by the bad. But what throws me the most is that he went to the trouble to putting this picture in a frame and sitting it where he spent the most time.

Unlocking the old workshop a few minutes later takes me on another unwitting trip down memory lane. It's an old garage on which Dad bricked up the wide door when he decided he needed a workshop more than Mom needed a place to park her car. Bad decision—maybe the beginning of the end for them, or at least an early indicator that her needs didn't come first. For me, though, it was—I'm forced to realize now—the place where I learned my trade.

It smells like old wood and sawdust, and I can see the remnants of Dad working here as recently as a few months ago. I load up the old black potbelly stove in the corner with some dry wood and kindling from a pile near the door, and am pleased to find out I still know how to build a fire even though the fireplace at my townhouse flips on with a switch.

Dad's collection of wood-carving tools still lines two drawers of the red Craftsman tool cabinet his father gave him on his twenty-first birthday, and their worn oak handles take me back. My tools are newer, maybe a little fancier—but these are dependable and familiar, the ones I learned with, my dad watching over me.

I also find enough spare scraps of cedar to make the box. Since I don't have the time to dovetail the joints, I mitre them instead. At the shop in town, so far I'm mostly just cutting and preparing the wood and haven't gotten to the actual building part yet, so this feels good. The level of concentration it takes relaxes me until I get a little lost in it, something I've always liked about carpentry. For me, it's a way to turn off the rest of the world—nothing matters but the project in front of you. And, as always, even with just a simple box, the act of seeing something evolve where it wasn't before is satisfying.

When the box is square and smooth, with the requested slot on top, it's time to create the magic she asked for, and that's where the carving tools come in. Opening one of the red drawers, I select a three-millimeter U-gouge and begin to free hand a curvy, curly design on one side. I like how it looks and keep going – it takes a while, but I carve out the swirls on all four sides and the top until it feels done. I picked up some primer and paint this morning before heading to the manor, and after a couple coats of snowy white, the box looks like it could have come straight from the North Pole.

I check the fire to see it's dying down, then clean up a little. Dad left things pretty sloppy, so I start stacking wood remnants—and that's when I spot one more thing that throws me. Resting on a shelf above the workbench is a little wooden sailboat so rudimentary it looks almost primitive in style. The wood remains bare but for a number eleven painted in blue on the wooden sail. It's the first little project I ever created out here. He wasn't even teaching me yet—it was more me hanging around when I was seven or eight, and him giving me a little pile of scraps, instructing me to see what I could make with it while he worked. I don't know why a sailboat came to mind, but through mimicking his sawing and cutting, whittling and carving, hammering and nailing, my crude little sailboat came into being.

And he kept it. All this time. He kept it.

I quit coming out here when he got mean, and the space holds both good memories and bad. But I can't deny that this is where the magic happened.

Sure, I roll my eyes at talk of "Christmas magic"—*magic* isn't a word usually in my vocabulary. But having learned how to take simple pieces of wood and turn them into something else—sometimes useful, sometimes beautiful, sometimes both...well maybe that *does* feel like a certain kind of magic.

I hadn't thought for a long time about the fact that it was Dad who taught me. When Lexi brought it up that first morning, for some reason I balked. Now I can see it, though. My dad didn't give me much, but he gave me a skill that has largely defined my life up to now. And it came with that means of escape, that way of shutting everything else out.

Not that I get to *use* the skill as much as I like these days—ever since my job has evolved into more of a management position. The act of making this box has reminded me that I miss what it used to be. I think I'll enjoy the cabinetry work in town in the coming weeks, too.

And Dad also gave me my truck, which I love. I coveted it growing up, and the day I got my license, he handed me the keys and said, "I know you'll take good care of it." By then, we were barely speaking and it shocked me.

"Don't look so surprised, boy," he said with a forced sort of laugh. "I know you've wanted it all your life—now it's yours."

I mumbled a stunned thanks and have been putting both heart and money into it ever since. While other guys I know take on huge car payments to own a Corvette or a Porsche, I wouldn't want to be behind the wheel of anything but my '48 Ford F-1. Another means of escape, this one more literal.

That's never hit me before—that he gave me, wittingly or not, everything I needed to get away from him.

When I pull the pickup to the snowy curb in front of the Lucas Building that night after dark, snow is falling again on an otherwise still, quiet street. The first thing my eyes land on? A familiar white mutt huddled under the overhang again. *Damn it, dog.*

When I came home last night, he'd done okay in the shop and it seemed too heartless to put him back out in the cold, so I let him stay overnight. This morning, I found a big pile of thank you.

Not that I'm sure what I expected the dog to do.

The Christmas Box

When ya gotta go and some idiot has trapped you inside a building, ya go. But I put him out this morning and had to drive away to the sounds of canine whimpering behind me.

Now I lean my face over into one hand. Do I not have enough on my mind without adding a stupid stray dog who can't seem to find any better shelter than this completely open-to-the-elements storefront?

Letting out a sigh, I get out and slam the old truck's door. I unlock the shop and carry Lexi's "wishing box" inside, while, of course, the dog scrambles in around my feet, nearly tripping me.

"You're lucky you didn't make me drop this box, dog," I mutter as I lower it to the counter in back.

Now what?

I could put his mangy carcass back outside, but it's really coming down out there again. What's with all this snow? While it's not rare to get an early December snowfall here every now and again, this is starting to feel more like Chicago than Kentucky.

I look down at the mutt, both disgusted and sympathetic. I haven't forgotten what it's like to feel abandoned and on your own. "But I knew where to go to the bathroom," I tell him accusingly. Damn, I must be tired, talking to a dog like I think he understands me. But the poor thing has sad eyes that get me in the gut.

And what's worse—I keep right on doing it. Though maybe I'm talking to myself now. If that's any better. "Maybe if I take you upstairs, give you some dinner, and put out some paper, you'll show your appreciation by pooping *there*." I saw an old pile of Winterberry Gazettes in the storage room in back.

A little while later, I've created a bathroom space for the mutt, and since I mostly stocked the small freezer with frozen microwave dinners, before I know it I'm heating him up his own chicken pot pie. "I can't believe I'm doing this," I say—to both of us, I guess.

But when I lower it to the floor and he scarfs it down like a maniac, I'm glad I did.

After eating my own pot pie, I find an old blanket and lay it out on the floor near a heat register. "There ya go," I say. "But don't get too comfortable—it's just for tonight."

December 5

Lexi

The Christmas Box is quiet—too quiet—but after another two inches of snow overnight, what do I expect? "I never thought I'd be mad about snow at Christmastime," I say to Dara, "but this needs to stop."

We stand side by side behind the long mahogany counter, sprucing up some signs we've just made.

"Don't worry," she says. "They've cleared the roads and it's still early—business will pick up." Then she motions to the sheet of white construction paper she's written on in tidy blue print. "What do you think?"

I take a look.

Instructions:

1. Drop your wish inside our wishing box.
2. Believe in Christmas magic.

I smile. "Yes," I say. "Perfect."

My own sign is bigger—with curly lettering on white poster board. The words *Wishing Box* and an arrow are surrounded by silver foil stars I cut out by hand. Dara also printed out slips of paper, with spots for a name and *My wish*, to place next to the box.

"Now all we need is the box." I have no idea when to expect it—I didn't specify a day, and I haven't a clue how long it will take, especially since Travis has plenty else to deal with right now. Plus, I still don't know if he can really be counted on for this. But I'm hoping it will show up soon. Maybe I'll drop in a wish for it to stop snowing already.

"Um, believe it or not," Dara says, "I think it's crossing the street right now."

Following her gaze, I find Travis Hutchins heading our way, carrying the most beautiful, intricately-carved wooden box I've ever seen. I rush from behind the bar to the door, holding it open for him. And the closer the box gets, the more breathtaking it becomes. I gasp at the sight.

"I believe you ordered a magical wishing box," he says, toting it across the threshold.

I'm truly awestruck and can't take my eyes off it. It's a hand-crafted piece of art. I'd think it was antique if I didn't know he just made it. Despite myself, I can't hide my reaction. "Travis, it's amazing! You made this in just the past couple of days? It looks like it belongs in an art gallery."

"So it's magical enough for you?"

I've cleared a small table for it, which I motion to. "It's *beyond* magical! Isn't it beyond magical, Dara?"

"Oh, completely beyond," she agrees, but I mainly think she's making fun of me.

As he lowers the gorgeous box to its new home, I remember my manners and ask, "Have you met my favorite employee, Dara Burch?"

"I'm your *only* employee," she reminds me, one brow arched in my direction.

I simply offer up a smile and a shrug.

"I think I've paid her for coffee a couple of times," Travis replies, glancing toward her, "but not officially. Travis Hutchins." He gives her a nod.

"Nice to meet you. And nice work on the box. It's putting a much-needed smile back on Lexi's face."

He swings his gaze in my direction. "What's wrong?"

Another shrug from me, probably a discouraged-looking one, and this time without the smile. "Guess I'm just hoping word will get out about our wishing box and then people will flock from far and wide to shop here."

He casts me a sidelong glance. "Wait a minute. This from the woman who lives on holiday cheer all year long? Don't tell me the Grinch snuck in and stole your Christmas."

"It so happens that you're the only Grinch I know, and you haven't stolen anything that I'm aware of." Well, if I don't count my Christmas laurel dreams. But I keep that to myself this time.

"Hey, I don't have to stoop to stealing Who hash and stuffing Christmas trees up chimneys to be Grinchy. But what happened to that holly jolly attitude of yours? I figured that was a twenty-four/seven kinda thing with you."

I consider inventing some sort of fib—still suffering a niggling desire to appear strong and successful in front of him, especially since he initially dissed my shop—but I go with honesty instead. "Listen, if I wake up looking on the bright side of life most days, it's because I *choose* to. It's a mindset that just makes life better. But as for me needing a smile...well, let's just say business better pick up fast for me to make a real go of it."

At this, he tilts his handsome head, appearing surprised. "Place seems busy most of the time."

I sigh. "It is. It just needs to be busier. I'm not on pace to clear what I need to by Christmas. And these last couple of snowy days haven't helped. It's keeping people indoors when they'd usually be out."

He tips his head back in understanding, then assures me, "Maybe things'll pick up. I can't imagine we'll have any more snow for a while."

That's when I notice a familiar-looking white dog pressing a wet nose against my plate-glass door. "Aw, look who it is." Then I take in its expression. "He seems sad."

Now it's Travis who suddenly appears grumpy—glancing toward the door to grouse, "Not you again."

"How'd it go when you let him in the shop the other night?" I ask.

"Well, turns out it's a her. And *she* pooped and peed."

I lower my chin a bit. "And you know it's a girl *how*?"

He lets out a sigh. "I was stupid enough to bring her in *again*, this time up to the apartment. I noticed she peed in a squatting position instead of cocking a leg like most male dogs, so I checked, and sure enough, she's a she. I put her

The Christmas Box

back out this morning, but apparently now she thinks she's mine."

I study the little dog through the glass. "She's really cute. And so sad-looking. Why don't you adopt her?"

He gapes at me like I just suggested he jump off the top of the Rockefeller Center Christmas tree. "Because I don't especially like dogs any more than I like Christmas. And again, she's pooped and peed on *both* levels of the Lucas Building now."

"Well, put down some padding or paper. Maybe she's paper-trained," I suggest.

"Tried that. Didn't work. Instead, she went directly *next* to the paper. Like she was taunting me."

I switch my focus from the dog to him. "Yes, I'm sure her goal is to torment you. And who doesn't like dogs? Even the Grinch had a dog. She could be your trusty companion. Frankly, you seem like a guy who could *use* a friend."

He looks affronted, his eyes going wide. "Don't worry about me—I have *plenty* of friends. They just don't happen to be in Winterberry."

I find myself wondering just what kind of friends he has, if I'd like them, and if any of them are female and come with benefits. But then I quickly close the door on that line of curiosity and, with a head tilt, I remember out loud, "You *were* kind of a loner, weren't you?"

He shrugs. "Not always. Just by high school, I guess. And I had a *few* buddies then—just not ones I kept in touch with."

I decide to turn things back to the cute furball outside

the door. "Well, you know what they say. A dog is man's best friend. And this one is ready to fill the role."

"Or *you* could adopt her," he suggests pushily, "if you like her so much." He arches a challenging brow in my direction.

But I glance back at the dog to find she has eyes only for Travis. "She's not mooning at *me* like I'm her long-lost BFF," I point out.

He shrugs before remarking, "I think *anyone* who gives her something to eat would rate best friend status."

"You should call her Marley," I go on anyway.

He looks suspicious. "Why?"

"Because Marley was besties with Scrooge."

"Very funny." It comes with an eye-roll.

I really do like the idea, though. "And Marley was a ghost in A Christmas Carol, and she's white, so I think it suits her."

"Well, you can call the mutt whatever you want, but she's still the town stray. The last thing I need right now is a dog."

Travis

I'm crossing back over to my side of the street after leaving the Christmas Box, and about the time I reach the door, I hear the blast of a horn and the skid of tires on wet asphalt. I spin to see a big Dodge Ram 3500, jacked up on chunky tires, come sliding to a halt just inches from the scruffy dog, who appears to have frozen in fright directly in the middle of Main Street while it was apparently following me home. My heart clenches.

"Oh God," I mutter, moving instinctively toward her. "Come here, girl. Come on!"

The silly dog finally gets hold of her senses and bounds toward me as a burly, bearded guy yells out the driver's side window, "Keep your dog out of the street, idiot!"

"She's not mine," I say, but too low for him to hear since it hardly matters.

He screeches off as I stoop down to the dog's level. She's shivering, so I pet her and try to calm her down. "You're okay, girl. You're all right," I hear myself cooing to her like I probably haven't to an animal since I was a kid. We always had some mutt or another around, but they were always doing things to make Dad yell at them—peeing on the floor, for instance. That's why I never liked them much—they seemed bound for trouble and gave Dad one more reason to be mad.

That's when I realize I'm just as shaken as Marley. I'm vigorously smoothing the damp fur on her head and neck with both hands, my heartbeat finally starting to slow down. Poor dog is wet and probably cold.

And then it hits me. I've started thinking of her as Marley, that fast.

This is all Lexi's fault.

When a drop of moisture lands on my cheek, I raise my gaze to see that it's started snowing again. Great, just great.

Then I look back to the dog and roll my eyes. "Guess this means you're coming in."

Lexi

I've taken it all in through the shop window. One minute I'm standing there admiring my beautiful new wishing box, and the next, I hear the squeal of tires outside. As the big pickup moves on, I let out a sigh of relief, reporting to Dara, "She's okay. She's okay. And...oh my God, he's stooping down, petting her...almost kind of hugging her. Maybe he's not a dog-hater, after all. Only..." That's when I notice something else. "Oh no. No, no, no. This can't be."

"What? What can't be?" comes her worried voice from across the store.

"It's snowing," I announce. "It's actually snowing. Again." I end on a sigh.

Dara walks up beside me, joining me to peer out on the suddenly-snowy doggie drama. Then she tosses me a suspicious sideways glance. "You like him."

I turn a you-can't-be-serious look her way. "Because I'm glad the dog didn't get hit by a monster truck means I like the guy who claims not to want the dog? Don't be ridiculous."

"No," she says. "You like him because...maybe you always did? Even back in high school? And now he's back and not as bad as you thought?"

She's fishing. Putting her small-town-detective cap on. But it's not working. "We have nothing in common," I point out.

She's on a roll now, though. "And that's why you asked him to build you a box, so you'd have a reason to see him again."

Now I roll my eyes. "I asked him to build me a box because he's, like, a master carpenter or something."

"You could have called Talc Brewsaugh," she points out. The carpenter who did all the work on the inside of the shop for me after I bought it.

"Talc stays busy, and it would have been a very small project for him. Travis was right across the street, and the obvious choice when I decided I needed a wishing box."

"Or maybe he's *why* you decided you needed a wishing box." She sounds so accusing. "Maybe it was subconscious. Maybe *you* don't even know you like him. *Yet.*"

I release a tired breath and shake my head. "I think I know what I like. And it's not the guy across the street, no matter how pretty that box turned out. I mean, he's not an awful person or anything, but...he's hardly my type. He's grouchy at least half the time. He has all this baggage with his dying father that he doesn't seem concerned about dealing with. And he's barely acknowledged what he did to me in high school. After all, you can't just say a few words —none of them sorry, by the way—and expect everything to be fine.

"And on top of all that, he hates Christmas. How could I, of all people, ever want to be with a guy who hates Christmas?"

December 7

Lexi

Okay, he hates Christmas, but...for some reason I still hold out hope.

Not because I'm into him like Dara thinks. But because I made that wish. On the star. The truth is, every time I see him—whether he's being gruff or nice—that wish comes back to me.

And something about that night, that moment, just felt...like someone somewhere was listening. God, the universe, angels—whoever makes such things happen. And sure, if I said that out loud to anyone, they'd think I was a loon. But I personally think miracles are all around us if we care to look. I think they happen every day—we just don't always know about them.

And despite all of Travis Hutchins' many flaws, I guess it just makes me sad when someone can't embrace the goodness of the season. The more I come to know about him, and about what's happening with his dad right now—well, I continue to think that he, more than most people, would really benefit from letting a little Christmas warmth into his life, believing in the magic.

Or...maybe I'm deluding myself. Maybe I want him to be someone he's just not. Someone who apologizes for his mistakes. Someone who cares about his dying father. Someone who *could* believe.

Or...maybe I'm just letting myself get wrapped up in this idea of wanting him to like Christmas because I'd rather think about *that* than the potential grim reality facing my brand new business? Maybe I'm distracting myself from my own problems, which I have no idea how to solve, by worrying about something I think I *can* fix? Though why I think that, I have no idea—that wish certainly hasn't shown any signs of coming true yet.

This morning, I'm standing in the same spot as last night when Marley nearly got hit by that truck, peering out the window. And just like then, it's snowing. It's snowed off and on all night. The streets are slushy and Main Street is depressingly still when Dara comes plodding up the snow-covered sidewalk in her fur-trimmed snowboots, bundled from head to toe.

"I probably should have called and told you not to come in," I say glumly as she pushes through the door, the bells jingling her arrival.

"I can go home if you want," she offers, "but the snow is supposed to end soon and it's Saturday, so I think people will come out anyway."

I gesture to the empty, quiet thoroughfare outside. "It's

ten o'clock, our lights are lit, our door is open, and no one's here." I let out a sigh and confide, "I thought…if I build it, they will come, you know? Like in that old Field of Dreams movie." I shake my head. "But if this is what a Saturday in December looks like, how empty will we be the rest of the year?" Maybe Travis was right and this was a stupid idea in the first place.

Unzipping her parka, she walks over to stand behind me and uses mittened hands to massage my shoulders in a pep-talky way. "Know what I think you need? To put a wish in your pretty new wishing box. Have you yet? Has anyone?"

I glance at it, now ready for business with ink pens and slips of paper. "No. Snow's kept everyone away since it showed up yesterday."

"Then I say we christen it," she suggests, pulling me toward it by one mitten.

I let out a thoughtful sigh, liking the idea. "Maybe you're right."

"You first," she says. "You dreamed up the idea—yours should be the very first one."

I fill out one of the little forms she created.

Name: Lexi
My wish: For the Christmas Box to be a grand success in every way.

Then I fold it in half and slip it through the slot on top.

I watch as Dara does the same, dropping hers inside as well—and then we share a smile.

"There," she says. "Didn't that feel good?"

I nod. "Thanks for suggesting it." Then I look around at the empty shop, all glistening and glowing for no one but the two people working there. "Now if only we had customers to make wishes, too."

After Dara gets the hot chocolate and coffee going, she wipes down the counter and is soon reduced to fluffing tree branches. Despite the cheerful holiday music playing, the place feels quiet and still. A few minutes later, she looks up from behind an artificial blue spruce to say, "Maybe I *should* go. I know you can't afford to pay someone when there's nothing to do."

It depresses me in more ways than one. The my-brand-new-business-failing way and also because I know she enjoys being here. She loves her mom very much, but got thrust into the role of full-time caregiver without much choice.

She's right, though—I have to be practical. I just give her a sad nod of agreement.

She heads to the back room where she stashes her coat, and when I see her through the doorway rewinding the scarf around her neck that she just took off a little while ago, the sight only adds to my sadness.

We need some joy around here, but where is it going to come from?

That's when I hear the slam of a door and glance outside to see Travis Hutchins' old red pickup rumble to life. The wipers swish powdery snow from his windshield and a few seconds later, the truck pulls away, leaving a snow-free rectangle behind. The Lucas Building looks drab and lifeless in the December chill, like Travis's bah-humbug attitude is somehow taking root in an old storefront I've always found perfectly charming until right now.

That's when it hits me for the first time that it's the only building on Main with no holiday decorations. No wonder it looks lackluster in comparison.

And as Dara starts back toward the door, rebundled, I say, "Wait."

This halts her in place. "Why?"

"I just came up with a plan."

She blinks. "A plan? About how to get more customers in the store?"

"No. About how to spread Christmas cheer. To Travis."

Her eyebrows shoot up. Understandably, since I've changed gears pretty fast there. But it surprises me when she says, "Whatever you're thinking, it's a terrible idea."

I push back. "How can you say that? You don't even know what it is."

"But what I do know is that if the guy's not into Christmas, that's his business. And maybe not something you should insert yourself into?"

I scrunch my nose up to tell her, "It just bothers me. He needs some Christmas joy in his life."

She sends me a knowing sideways glance. "Like I said yesterday, you like him."

"Do not," I argue with the all the maturity of a fifth grader.

"And that's why you care about how he feels."

"I care about how *everyone* feels," I claim, letting my gaze widen to punctuate the statement. "This just happens to be the person in front of me at the moment, the person who needs some merriness. And maybe I don't need his *lack* of merriness bringing me down. There's enough to worry about without having a Christmas hater right outside my window."

Even as her eye roll tells me she's not buying it, she asks, "Well, I still think drumming up business would be a much better use of your energy, but what are we doing to de-Scrooge the unsuspecting guy across the street?"

"I can't believe you talked me into this," Dara says.

She's carrying the top of the fake Christmas tree and I'm toting the wider bottom. We're lugging it up the old metal stairway that runs along the outside rear of the Lucas Building. Which is snow-covered. Which I didn't factor in to this. So it's a little treacherous, but we're careful and make it up okay.

The door to the apartment is unlocked. Which I *did* factor in and got lucky with. I'm not sure Travis ever even uses this door, but I happen to know Wally and Edie never locked it back when the furnished apartment upstairs was vacant, just in case someone needed to drop something off after business hours.

As the two of us drag the tree inside, we're met by a familiar white dog. "Marley!" I say in greeting. "Well, well, well—looks like your brush with death got you a home." I feel smugly victorious. "And he claims he doesn't like dogs."

She's wagging her tail, clearly happy to see us, too. But she's also peed on the floor, which I decide I'll clean up before I leave. One less black mark against her with Travis.

"Um, where are we going with this thing?" Dara asks.

"Sorry—got sidetracked there." I scan the small studio apartment and see the perfect spot. "In front of the windows." Three connected sash windows line the front of the old building, providing a nice view of Main Street.

After we get the tree set upright—one that came conveniently in one piece, no assembly required—Dara asks, "Okay, what next?"

"You go back for lights and ornaments, and I'll clean up the dog pee. Unless you'd rather swap tasks."

"Nope, lights and ornament-fetching it is. I'm on it."

Ten minutes later, the floor is clean and dry, I'm trying to school the dog on using the paper Travis has set out, and Dara is wrapping twinkling colored lights around the six-foot artificial Norwegian spruce.

She grabbed simple garden-variety ornaments—packages of colored glass balls—which I walk over and join her in hanging.

"I can't believe we're doing this," she says doubtfully.

But I just shrug. "It's the opposite of being a Grinch. He *stole* Christmas trees—I deliver them instead."

"Only I don't think Travis *wants* a Christmas tree," she insists on reminding me.

"*Or*," I say, "maybe he doesn't *know* he wants a Christmas tree. But now that it's here, who wouldn't enjoy it? Some lights will make *my* view nicer from across the street anyway." As a final touch, I arrange a red, knitted tree skirt around the bottom. After which I move a few steps back and take in our handiwork with pride.

Dara lets out a sigh. "It *is* cheerful." Then she glances out the window. "Hey, it stopped snowing and the sun is actually out. And—oh my God."

"Is he back?" I ask, rushing closer. "Please tell me he's not back."

"No, over there!" She points across the street to the Christmas Box, where no less than seven people are standing outside the door, clearly trying to get in and wondering why it's locked at this hour.

"We can't let 'em get away!" I declare. "You grab the ornament boxes and make sure Marley doesn't get out while I dash back to the shop!"

"Don't slip on the steps!" she calls as I fly out the door.

I nearly do, but catch myself, then scurry the rest of the way down.

Emerging from the narrow alley between the Lucas Building and the antique mall, I see that now cars line Main Street and Saturday shopping has indeed commenced. "Ladies," I call. "Sorry you had to wait—I ran an errand, but I'm so glad to see you all!"

"Well," says Marianne Jorgensen, an older woman I've known my whole life, "I heard you had some kind of a special box to put wishes in, so I brought my grandkids." Indeed, the two little ones, a boy and girl of around five or six, are peering eagerly in the window as if expecting to catch a glimpse of Santa.

"We heard about the box, too." Wendy Acara, still looking as blond and pretty as in high school, is with her older sister and niece.

"How did you guys find out about it?" I ask, unlocking the door. I have no idea how word got out so quickly.

Marianne says, "I was visiting my mother at Bluegrass Manor and some of the nurses were chatting about it." Hmm, maybe Travis mentioned it to Helen?

And Wendy replies, "My mom was talking to Mrs. Burch on the phone last night and said Dara was raving about it."

Holding the door open to usher them all in, I say, "Come in, come in! The wishing box is right over there by the mantel." I point. The "And feel free to grab some coffee or cocoa on the house since I kept you waiting."

By the time Dara is back five minutes later, wishes are being made, hot chocolate poured, and purchases gathered. Wendy Acara's arms are loaded down before I can even offer to hold her selections behind the counter until she's ready.

"Lexi, this shop is adorbs," she says. "I've been meaning to check it out and I'm so glad I did. And that box is beautiful. What an awesome idea."

"Feel free to spread the word," I tell her loudly enough for other shoppers to hear. A few more have arrived and found their way to the box, as well. "When it comes to making wishes, the more the merrier."

"Let me at it," a laughing forty-something mom with her college-age daughter says. "I've got so many things to wish for, I might be here all day!"

That's when her daughter announces, "Mom, I have to have this," pointing to a fleecy Rudolph blanket. "And that snowman figurine." She points. "We have to get that for Mimi."

"Good thing I didn't go home," Dara says to me under her breath as she ditches her coat and hat behind the bar. "The rush to make wishes is on and you're officially a genius." She starts toward the register as several shoppers head in that direction while still more walk in the door.

And though I don't know if I'd go that far, I'd at least say things are looking up. Maybe the wish I put in the box just a little while ago is already starting to come true. And maybe my wish upon a star will, too?

That night I'm curled up in my PJs watching Elf in my apartment upstairs. Sitting with me on the couch is my beloved teddy bear, Crinkle. A gift from my grandma when I was very young, he wears a red, fur-trimmed Santa coat and, as the story goes, was introduced to me as Kringle, but apparently my four-year-old brain heard Crinkle. And Crinkle he has been ever since. I'm treating myself to a star-shaped sugar cookie from Janie's Bakery as I watch Buddy the Elf walk across the candy cane forest and through the Lincoln Tunnel, and I'm also…keeping an occasional eye out the window for Travis's truck. He's been gone all day.

Not that I'm keeping tabs on him or anything.

It's certainly none of my business where he is or what he's doing.

But when finally I hear the familiar rumble of the old Ford, along with the slam of its door, I peek out to see Travis going inside. The Christmas tree Dara and I snuck in this morning has been shimmering in the second-floor window all day, and now that darkness has fallen, it adds to the cheer of all the other holiday lights up and down Main. And frankly, I'm glad it's there to provide some light for Marley. Only, wow, I wonder how many times she's gone to the bathroom by now, probably not on the paper.

The movie continues, but my mind stays across the street. I imagine him walking up the stairs, emerging into the apartment to be greeted by the happy glow of a Christmas tree. I envision him feeling warmly toward me for doing it, and then deciding maybe Christmas isn't so bad after all.

That's when an interior light illuminates his apartment. And the Christmas tree lights promptly go out.

Just like that.

My heart sinks.

Why was I so foolish to think he'd respond the way... well, the way most people would? He's not most people. I guess I was wrong and that particular wish isn't coming true, after all, and my distraction was...just a distraction. So much for Operation Wish Upon a Star.

December 8

Lexi

I'm outside clearing the sidewalk of leftover slush, grateful for yesterday's increase in business, but sad that Travis still hasn't seen the light. Or the *lights*—literally. When I think of him turning off the tree lights while his others stayed on for hours afterward—I just happened to notice—I can only draw one conclusion: He really *is* a Grade A Grinch. Christmas magic is not going to darken *his* door—he's firmly committed to that.

I go back inside with an hour to spare before we open, and with time on my hands, I start the coffee since I could use a cup after not sleeping particularly well last night.

Then my eyes fall on the wishing box across the room. Every person who came in yesterday left a wish inside. Some had heard about it through the Winterberry grapevine and others only found out about it upon happening in, but everyone loved making their wishes. And so the thing that felt "missing" from the shop was indeed that little spark of magic, and this beautiful box filled the void.

After the coffee brews, I pour some into a mug circled with reindeer leading Santa's sleigh, and I take heart that at least *some* people can embrace the holidays.

When the sleighbells on the door suddenly jangle like they've been hit with gale force winds, I flinch, sloshing a little hot coffee on my hand, and look up to see the box maker himself.

Uh oh. I try to ignore the angry look on his face, along with the seething pain on my skin, as I announce cheerfully, "Great news! The wishing box is a hit! People are talking about it all over town!"

"Swell," he says dryly, sliding onto a stool at the coffee bar. "Give me my free coffee."

"Hang on a minute," I say, because the burn stings. I set my cup down, then dash to the sink, running cold water over my hand. "I burned myself when you came barreling in here like a madman."

"Oh. Sorry." He actually sounds concerned, like maybe my injury defused his anger a little.

Though I assure him, "It'll be fine," as I grab up his usual green-speckled Santa mug and pour his coffee. Maybe I should have milked the burn more, but I've decided I might as well get to the matter at hand. Sliding the cup his way, I venture cautiously, "You seem... unhappy."

He arches a menacing brow in my direction before

growling, "I remember when you could leave your door unlocked in this town."

Nibbling my lower lip nervously, I ask, "Um, what happened? Did you have a break-in? A burglary?" I'm suddenly regretting my impulsive tree delivery. It seemed like such a cheerful idea at the time.

"Worse," he snarls at me. "Some holiday-crazed, rogue decorator took it upon herself to come into my private space and erect a full-size Christmas tree, complete with blinking lights." He continues to appear extremely put out with me.

I'm sure I look guilty. "To be fair, it's actually more of a sparkling effect. But there's a bulb you can switch out to make it stop."

He looks at me like I might be crazy. "That's only *one* of the many problems with this situation. Another is that you knew I wouldn't want a Christmas tree."

"It's...for Marley," I claim, however lamely. "In A Christmas Carol, Marley wanted Scrooge to embrace the spirit of the season. Marley understood what it was all about and just wanted his buddy to get it, too."

He tilts me a look. "Well, the Marley at my place just wants food and shelter and isn't too picky about anything else."

Meanwhile, I'm still lip-nibbling. "I cleaned up some dog pee while I was there if that helps at all."

In response, he holds up his index finger and thumb, close together, as if silently saying: a little. But there's still not even a hint of a smile on his face as he finally picks up his mug. "I can't believe you just came into my place. I mean, how would you like it if I just helped myself into *your* apartment?"

Okay, the truth is, I'm not sure I would mind. Which is a very bad sign and may mean Dara is right about me being attracted to him. Because I *should* find the very notion outrageous. A realization that makes me understand where he's coming from. Okay, I overstepped.

"You're right," I say. "I'm sorry. I didn't mean to invade your privacy. And I promise it was a quick in and out—I just put up the tree, cleaned up the pee, and left. It was an impulsive act, which I can now see wasn't a good idea. Can you forgive me?"

He looks calmer now, drinking his coffee, perhaps thrown by my earnest apology—but at the same time I can also see the wheels spinning in his head. They're spinning in mine, too. I've just apologized to a guy who's owed me an apology for a dozen years and still hasn't given it.

"Yeah," he says slowly, meeting my gaze. "If...*you* can forgive *me*."

Ah, maybe he *does* see the light, at least this particular one.

"For?" I'm not just playing dumb this time, though—I'm making sure we're both thinking about the same transgression.

"High school. That dance. I'm sorry I wasn't big enough to do the right thing back then."

I take a deep breath, then let it back out, shocked by how much the words affect me. They've been a long time coming. And it's something I should have completely moved past ages ago. But I guess things that happen to us when we're young can have a lasting impact. Maybe I've needed this apology all this time without really knowing it—and here it finally is.

"Well, you were a punk," I remind him softly. "I appreciate the apology, and yes, I can forgive you." Though maybe I already had? I mean, despite what I keep telling myself, do you really go making wishes on stars for guys you haven't forgiven? Or sneaking trees into their apartments? Or letting it warm your heart when you see them hug a dog?

"Then we're good?" he asks, downing the last of his coffee.

I offer up a short nod. I could take him to task more; I could confess how much that night wounded my tender teenage heart—yet I understand many people find it hard to apologize and I suspect he's one of them, so I'll let him off the hook and put it behind me.

"But just so you know," he adds, "I still couldn't care less about having a Christmas tree, so I'm afraid you wasted your time there."

I just shake my head and inform him, "Kindness—or *attempted* kindness in this case—is never wasted."

"Whatever you say," he tells me, lowering his empty mug to the bar and rising from his stool. "You have a good day, Lexi."

I lift my hand in a small wave, then watch him go. He's always telling me to have a good day, or night—but I'd have better ones if he'd drop his guard just a little, just enough to let my wish for him come true.

After a brisk day of business, during which a steady stream of customers put wishes in the wishing box and left with shopping bags filled with gifts and decorations, I head upstairs to take a long, hot bath. Then I slip into a cozy pair of snowflake-laden pajamas, and soon enough find myself on the couch, watching a holiday rom-com—and glancing out at the windows across the street.

His truck is there. And the faint glow of a lamp dimly illuminates the second floor.

So what is it I'm waiting for?

The tree lights. I'm still hoping against hope that I'll see the Christmas tree lights come on. I keep thinking maybe, just maybe, something will suddenly compel him to plug them in.

I wait all evening to see the happy twinkle of colored lights in his windows.

But it never happens.

December 9

Travis

I spend the day doing detail work on the soap shelves, which are turning out well. The dog keeps me company, and following some advice from the internet, I put her on a leash I picked up yesterday, keeping her confined to the area near the layered "puppy pads" I also bought, to replace the newspaper. Each time I see her start to go, I guide her over. So far, she's not really catching on, but at least I have less messes to clean up.

Late in the day, I pick up some burgers and head to the manor.

Once there, I pop in on Shannon and ask if she needs anything moved today. She shakes her head and looks at me like I'm a moron and why would I think she needed anything moved?

Then I take Dad his usual hamburger and fries—and all hell breaks loose.

"Here you go," I say, holding the bag up as I walk into his room. "Medium well and greasy, just the way you like it."

"Who are you and why are you trying to poison me?" he asks.

I just gape at him, dumbfounded. He's thrown me off yet again.

At a loss, my heart sinking in my chest, I simply turn back around, exit the room, and head to the nurse's station. Without preamble, I announce at large, "My father just asked me who I am and accused me of trying to poison him."

Helen looks up from the computer screen she's studying, her expression troubled. "Oh dear. I was hoping to see you come in so I could warn you. He's not himself today."

Or maybe he's back to his *old* self. But I don't tell her that.

"He's not recognizing anyone, I'm afraid."

"Is this a sign of progression? Of the brain cancer?" Something in me stiffens as I ask, though. Despite myself, maybe I *have* started liking this guy I don't really know anymore. And maybe I'm not ready for him to disappear just yet, especially if it means dealing with a mean, nasty guy going forward. Coming here sucks, but being met with a smile each day has at least made it tolerable.

"Yes and no," she tells me. "Certainly, it's indicative of progression, but we had days like this before you got to town, too. His cognition is unpredictable. And maybe that will grow more prevalent over time or maybe it won't.

When it comes to diseases like this, every journey is different, so I don't try to predict what'll happen next."

I draw in a deep breath and blow it back out, again stunned to realize how much I want today to be just an anomaly, and how wounded I was by his hateful tone. It felt like being seventeen all over again, something I never expected. Steeling myself as best I can, I ask, "What should I do? Leave and hope he's better tomorrow?"

She tilts her head in that calm, thoughtful way of hers. "That's up to you, Travis. But if it were me, I'd probably take the food back in and try to reason with him, just remembering that he's not in control of his own mind right now. If it's too much, then leave. But maybe give it another shot."

I sigh. Helen has a flair for pushing a person to do the right thing. Because I definitely want to take off, get away from this situation. I'd much rather be at the apartment with my dog and my Christmas tree, neither of which I like very much, so that's saying a lot. But I finally murmur, "Okay," and head back to Dad's room, each step filled with dread.

"I said, 'Who are you?'" He repeats when I come back in, as if no time has passed at all.

"I'm your son," I inform him, perhaps a little too forcefully. Maybe I should be gentler, more understanding, but this is jarring

"My son lives far away and never comes home," he tells me, "so you ain't him."

Where to go from here? "Well, I brought you lunch

from Winterburger if you want it." I'm back to holding up the bag.

"That nurse tried to poison me earlier. Saw her put something in my scrambled eggs. I refused to eat it, I'll tell ya that much."

Do you try to correct someone at a time like this, or do you just move on? Without any training in this area, I'm stumped. "Look," I say, "I have two hamburgers and some fries here, and I'm gonna eat one of 'em. You can pick which one if you want. That makes it safe, right? And if you don't want yours, I have a dog at home who'll be more than happy to eat it."

"You have a dog?" he asks with the sudden wonder of a child.

And that's when I realize: Crap, I just said I had a dog. Which I guess means I have one. Again, I blame Lexi for this.

That woman has intruded into more than just my private space—she's managed to meddle in multiple aspects of my life. She's lucky she makes good coffee or I'd be avoiding her like the plague. Of course, she has a pretty smile, too. And warm blue eyes. I'm seriously not sure why I didn't notice her in high school—how cute she is, I mean. And even though I never thought I cared about anything like this, I guess the way she looks on the bright side of life makes her...well, nice to be around. When she's not forcing dogs and Christmas trees on me, that is.

"I miss my dog," Dad announces then, drawing me back to the moment at hand.

He doesn't *have* a dog, but I don't tell him that since I'm still not sure of the proper way to handle his delusions. I could use Helen right about now. "What's your dog's name?" I ask.

"Blinker. He's a good boy."

Ah. Wally mentioned years back that Dad had taken in a stray, a little beagle, and called him Blinker. Apparently that's what we Hutchins men do, take in strays. Strange for two guys I don't think of as having big hearts. I'm pretty sure the beagle got old and passed away since then, so I guess Dad is in another place in time.

"Maybe you'll see him again soon," I suggest. I'm not sure what I even mean by that, but maybe I'm suggesting some form of an afterlife I have no idea if I believe in.

"Don't think so," he says sadly. "They don't let you bring your dog with you in here."

As I'm busy unpacking the bag, Dad snatches up one of the burgers, unwraps it, and starts eating like poison doesn't exist. I'm relieved but confused.

"Wow, this is a good burger," he says as if he hasn't had one every day since I got here. "What did you say your name was again?"

"Travis," I answer.

"That's my son's name."

Rather than get sucked into some kind of Abbot and Costello Who's On First conversation with him, I let it go and just eat.

Twenty minutes of confusing conversation later, I'm mentally exhausted and decide to leave. Once I'm out the door of dad's room, I'm eager to reach daylight. I don't say goodbye to anyone at the nurse's station—instead I'm bobbing and weaving between wheelchairs like a man possessed, the door within sight.

That's when my eyes fall on Dottie, the old woman always cradling the babydoll. She looks up at me from her wheelchair with her usual sad expression, but this time I see a tear roll down her wrinkled cheek. That's a first, and a disturbing one.

I want to keep walking; I'm desperate to get out of here. But her eyes get to me, same as they have since the moment I first encountered her.

It's then that I realize she doesn't have her doll. Another first.

"What's wrong, Dottie?" I ask even though I've never heard her speak.

With anguish still spilling from her gaze, she points up the hall.

I turn to see a dark-haired man padding along in slippers and yet another saggy robe. The babydoll dangles from his hand—he's holding it by the ankle.

The sight ignites a fire in my chest. I've never been a parent, and I've never suffered from dementia, but I instinctively feel Dottie's horror at what she thinks is happening to her baby. I march up to the guy, placing my hand on his shoulder to spin him roughly around.

Once he regains his footing, he gives me a little smile that strikes me as smug, mocking.

"That's not yours," I growl, snatching the doll from his hand. "Don't let me catch you bothering her again. Got it?"

To my surprise, nothing about his attitude changes—he's still giving me that weird little smile. We standing face

The Christmas Box

to face, me feeling like I'm about to explode and him looking cool as a cucumber.

That's when a touch comes on my arm and I turn to see Helen. "Travis," she says gently, "he doesn't mean any harm. He doesn't know what he's doing."

Oh my God. Of course he doesn't. It wasn't a mocking smile—it was a docile one. Why did it take Helen to make me see that? Nothing here is predictable; no one here is as you'd expect them to be. But even after a trip through the Twilight Zone with Dad, I'm still slow on the uptake. And part of me wants to protest the situation, complain that Dottie shouldn't have to put up with this, that this guy should be locked up in his room—but I already know that's not right, either.

I'm sure Helen can see my response in my eyes, but I say nothing in reply—I just walk the babydoll back to where Dottie still sits in her wheelchair. I hand it down to her and watch her hug it to her chest as if I have, indeed, just given her back her abducted child.

"She thinks its real," Helen says quietly, stepping up next to me.

"I know. That's why I had to get it back for her."

"She lost a baby girl in an accident when she was young and never had more children."

Oh, good—this just went from sad to tragic. Makes a guy with brain cancer who misses his dog seem like child's play.

"Thank you for helping her—we try, but we can't be everywhere at once. We've been short-handed for a while now—we have openings, but no one to take them."

I don't blame anyone for not wanting this job, but of course I'm not going to tell her that. She's a saint. Instead I just say, "I gotta go."

"I know it's hard," she says, squeezing my hand before I start toward the door.

I've never felt freer than I do stepping out into the cold, wintry air, sucking it deep into my lungs. But my heart hurts when I think of all the people inside who can't just walk away.

Lexi

Most of Main Street closes on Monday—it's pretty much me, Janie's, and Winterburger that bother to open. So today was a slower day, and one of Dara's off days. I like to envision a time when I'll close on Mondays, too, but that time is not now—now is when every sale counts.

After turning off the overhead lights to leave the shop illuminated by only the ones on the artificial trees and those lining the windows, I step outside and sit down on a park bench out front. Darkness has fallen on a clear, crisp December night and I want to breathe in some fresh air for a few minutes. My whole life now is inside the building behind me—I live there and I work there. Convenient, yes, but maybe I didn't factor in what life would be like never having to go anywhere. Other than a recent trip for groceries, I'm not even sure when I last drove my car, which stays parked out back.

A glance at the Lucas Building reminds me of the guy

who won't plug in a Christmas tree, but I'm glad he didn't stay mad at me.

And speak—or think—of the devil, that's when a familiar red pickup comes rolling up to the curb across the street.

As he steps out, I call across to him, "Mr. Scrooge, I presume?"

He slants me a look in the shadows from streetlights. "And if it's not Mrs. Claus, the Christmas queen herself."

I just offer up a small smile.

"I better not find any boughs of holly decking my halls when I go inside or you're in trouble."

"Nope," I tell him. "I've learned my lesson and stayed on my side of the street today."

"That's good to hear."

"Can I interest you in some free hot chocolate? Slow day and I'm about to throw it out when I go back inside."

I'm not even sure why I asked, and I expect him to say no. He looks like he's going to, hesitating. But then he shrugs. "What the hell—why not?" And starts in my direction.

My skin ripples slightly beneath my parka, and as much as I still want to think Dara is wrong about me being into him, I'm worried she's right. Which is a nightmare. Polar opposites and all that.

Inside, I turn the lights back on and get him a mug of cocoa. "Whipped cream?" I ask as he takes a stool. "Tiny marshmallows? A peppermint stick? We have a whole little shelf of fun add-ons over here."

He shakes his head. "None of that—I take it straight."

It draws a smile from me. "Of course you do. God forbid you get festive with your hot chocolate—someone might accuse you of being jolly."

"No threat of that happening anytime soon," he says with a small, self-aware smile.

After I make myself a cup, too, spraying a dollop of whipped cream on top and adding a few sprinkles for fun, I turn to him.

"Should we toast?" he asks, lifting his usual green Santa mug.

The simple suggestion surprises me. I don't point out that they're possibly the merriest three words I've ever heard my Scroogy neighbor speak, and instead reply, "Only if I get to decide what we toast to."

He rolls his eyes teasingly, somehow getting more handsome to me all the time. "That feels dangerous. But have at it."

It takes me only a few seconds to come up with the perfect thing. "To wishes," I say. "In boxes and on stars."

He bumps his mug against the candy-cane striped one I'm holding and says, "I guess that's not *too* bad. To wishes then." After which he glances across the shop to the white box. "So you say people are into this, huh?"

I nod. "Got a few more wishes today, in fact. I don't think anyone has come in since the box arrived who hasn't put one inside."

"Well, I'm glad it's what you wanted it to be."

"You should put a wish in, too," I tell him.

He looks like I've made an outrageous proposal. "Me? I don't think so."

"Why not? You just toasted to wishes."

He shrugs. "That was because I was thankful you hadn't toasted flying reindeer or snowmen coming to life when you put old hats on their heads," he tells me with a grin I feel in my solar plexus.

But he should know by now that it's going to take more than that for me to give up such a good idea. "Seriously," I persist. "What would be the harm in writing down a wish and dropping it inside? Everyone wishes for *something*, whether you write it down or not."

He lowers his chin, looking as if he's about to tell me a secret. "I'm afraid you wouldn't approve of anything I'd wish for."

"Like what?" I challenge him.

"Hmm." He plants one elbow on the counter and props his chin on top. "That the Christmas Box lady would quit trying to make me wish for silly things when I choose to live in reality? Or that my dad would bite the dust already so I can get back to my real life?"

I flinch at that last part—it's impossible not to.

"See?" he says. "I can still be a jerk."

I almost protest—maybe because I just don't want it to be true. He took in Marley, after all. I've seen the good in him. There's got to be more to this story. So instead I ask, "Why do you feel that way? About your dad."

He takes a drink of his hot chocolate while narrowing a suspicious gaze on me. "What, are you gonna psychoanalyze me now? Pursuing therapy as a fallback position?"

"I'm just curious," I explain. "I mean...I'd have given anything to grow up with a dad."

"But you're forgetting something," he says, pointing a finger my way. "Not all dads are created equal. If you'd had mine, you might wish you had none at all. *There's* a wish for you—I could put *that* one in the box."

Despite the harsh answer, I counter, "If he's so awful, why are you at the manor every day? I mean, surely you could be here doing your duty without going *that* often."

He takes a moment before telling me, "He's...a different guy now. Closer to how I remember him being when I was a little kid. I'm guessing it's the brain cancer mixing things up. But just a little while ago, he was all over the place—didn't even recognize me. And I guess it just reminded me of the bad old days."

"What was so bad about him?" I ask softly. "Back then."

At first I think he's not going to answer. I'm prying, after all, and I know it. And he doesn't seem like a guy who opens up to just anyone—and maybe, in fact, no one.

But after a minute, he says, "Okay, here's a for instance. I'm thirteen years old, the grandparents and cousins are over, and we're hosting Christmas dinner. My grandfather on my dad's side, who could also be kind of an ass, says, 'This turkey's too little. Ain't gonna have no leftovers.' My mother says she got the biggest one we could afford this year with dad out of work. And that insults my dad, so much that he stands up, starts raving about how he's doing the best he can but she's never satisfied, and he keeps right on going until he's picking up the gravy boat and sending it flying across the room to shatter into pieces against the kitchen wall.

"Everybody freezes—except me. I go start cleaning up the mess—just trying to somehow fix the situation. But then he yells at *me*—tells me to sit back down, that *she'll* clean it up. And then he and I end up in each other's faces—until Uncle Wally gets between us and calms things down.

"The upshot was—everyone left and I locked myself in my room the rest of the night. The mess was still there the next morning—I knew she wasn't gonna clean it up, on principle. So I did—but I caught hell for it later, from *both* of them if you can believe that."

I tilt my head as understanding dawns. "Oh. I get it now. That's why you hate Christmas."

But he only shoots me an annoyed look. "Of course you'd bring it around to that, but no, that's not *why I hate Christmas*." He mimics me.

I'm wholly unconvinced, though, and slant him a look right back. "Are you sure? I mean, if that happened to me, who knows, maybe *I'd* even hate Christmas."

"Well," he admits, thinking it through, "it *was* always worse then. The fighting. There were money troubles, like I said, and the holidays shine a light on that. And Christmas puts people on edge—so many expectations—so when you're already in a tense situation, the holidays just amplify it.

"After she was gone, we kind of just quit having Christmas altogether. Wally and Edie would invite us over, and Dad would go, but I refused. I didn't want anything to do with it."

I'm pretty horrified by all he's just said—he's right that not everyone's home lives growing up are the same. But I'm afraid if I tell him how sorry I am he went through that, he'll realize how much he just confided in me. So instead I move on to, "So you're telling me you don't think any of this is connected to your feelings about Christmas?" I slant him a knowing look.

Yet rather than answer, he turns it around and says, "Can I ask you something personal?"

Given everything he's just shared, I reply, "Sure."

"I know your memories of Christmas with your family are good ones. But...isn't it hard without them? To keep enjoying it so much? I mean, I lost my dad—in a way—when I was twelve and the construction outfit he worked for went belly up. This was back before he started his own business—he was out of a job with no warning. Money was tight, he took to drinking, it eventually drove my mom away—and nothing was ever the same after that, Christmas or anything else. You lost *your* dad, and then your mom and grandma, so I'm sure *your* Christmases aren't what they used to be, either. How do you keep loving it the way you do?"

For some reason, the question makes me feel vulnerable, an emotion I thought I'd long ago outgrown. Maybe because I'm about to tell him something I haven't told many people. I do it almost bashfully, from beneath lowered eyelids. "The holidays *were* hard for me afterward. But sometimes 'fake it 'til you make it' is good advice. You just pretend to feel a certain way until you really feel it."

He looks confused. "Are you telling me you *don't* really love Christmas?"

"Of course not!" I object as if he's suggested something preposterous.

"Thank God," he says, "because you were about to blow my entire worldview to bits."

"What I'm telling you is that it took a while," I explain. "It took remembering the good times, but accepting that those days were over and figuring out how to make *new* good times. It took finding my way. And it's not perfect. Believe it or not, even *I* have moments during the holidays when I feel a little down. You're right—there *is* a lot of expectation and buildup.

"But what I came to realize is that Christmas is...whatever you make it. You can dwell on hard memories and things that aren't what you want them to be—or you can focus on everything good and warm and uplifting about the season. For me, it's become about things like hope. And giving. And wishing. Like all the wishes in the box. Wishing keeps hope alive. And Christmas keeps wishing alive. And wishes are prayers. So even if Christmastime isn't perfect, I still think it's the most wonderful time of the year—not just because a song says so."

Travis

I cross the street a little while later, thinking about my conversation with Lexi. Sure, she'd told me about losing her mom and grandma before, but maybe this is the first time I'm realizing she has struggles, too. She sure handles them differently than I do, though. It's hard not to admire the way she just moves forward through it all, still seeing the good in every day.

What happened at the manor still has me on edge, though. Hot chocolate and talking with Lexi was...well, a nice balm after that—I'm glad I took her up on the invitation. But no amount of cocoa can fix what happened this afternoon.

Climbing the stairs to the apartment, I flip on a light and greet the dog. "Hey, girl," I say as she comes trotting over, tail wagging a thousand miles an hour. I bend over, scratching and nuzzling her. "Yes, you missed me, I see that," I tell her in a silly voice I'm not sure I've ever used before. I'll have to get better about leaving lights on for her if I won't be back before dark. "Bet you're ready for supper, huh?"

I need to pick up a sack of dog food, but for now, I start breaking some deli turkey from the fridge into bite size pieces in a bowl.

It's then that I notice her beginning to squat. "No," I say quickly. "No, no." I point to the puppy pad. "Paper," I say. "Go on the paper."

And that's when something downright shocking happens. She trots across the room and goes on the paper.

"Oh my God," I whisper. Then I walk over and stoop down beside her. "Good girl! Such a good girl. You did it—you really did it. It's a miracle. What a good girl you are."

And then I remember: treat! I'm supposed to give her a treat when she does it. I even bought some little doggie snacks just for this purpose—so I rush to the kitchen counter, grab one out of a box, and hold it down for her to take from me. "That's for being such a good girl."

I'm still petting her when I realize the word I just used. Miracle. I was kidding, exaggerating—but hell, what do I know? "Maybe Lexi's right and Christmas miracles really do exist," I murmur. "Maybe every single good thing that happens, in a way, is a miracle."

Then I catch myself. I'm holding Marley's face between my hands. And I've just told a dog I believe in miracles because she peed on the pad. I must be losing it. "I take it back," I tell the pooch. "It's not a miracle that you used the puppy pad. You're clearly just a very smart, trainable dog."

December 10

Lexi

The sign on the shop door says *Open*, but Main Street is dead.

Why? It's snowing again. Just when most of what had fallen so far has melted, more's coming down. I can't believe it.

But I'm looking on the bright side. Even though I kept an eye out for Travis's tree lights last night after our heart-to-heart and none came on, I still feel optimistic. Maybe he'll never love Christmas the way I do, but at least now I understand why. And I still believe in my wish for him. I know he can come to appreciate Christmas again—somehow.

And further looking on the bright side: Maybe it's actually good—in a way—that the store is empty, because I have a project to do. I've put it off and today is the deadline. I need to make a gingerbread house.

I've left it until the last minute because I've never actually built one before. Most Winterberrians would be shocked to find that out—I'm the Christmas lady, after all. And while I've baked some gingerbread men in my past, I've just never gotten into the homebuilding aspect of gingerbread. So I've bought two kits—allowing room for error—and that's how I plan to spend this quiet, snowy day.

After I put on a pot of coffee and get the Christmas music going, I step behind the counter and open up the first box, containing gingerbread panels, icing with a piping bag, red and green fondant, colored gum drops, and some candy beads. On a sturdy cardboard base, I begin to build.

Or I try to anyway. It looks sloppy from the start.

But I keep going, attempting to piece together a house with my panels and icing.

Eventually, I take it apart and start again. But it doesn't go much better. The cookie sheets seem too heavy to use as a roof—the whole thing keeps collapsing. I built sturdier houses of playing cards as a kid.

I'm to the point of frustration by the time the sleighbells announce a visitor and I look up to see Travis. "Coffee ready?"

I nod. "You'll have to get it yourself, though—I'm up to my elbows in icing here."

Yet I'd be perfectly happy to set it aside. There's a gingerbread event this evening, but maybe I won't go. Or I could show up empty-handed, but again, being the Christmas lady comes with a certain...is *mystique* too strong of a word?—I'm not sure I'm ready to dispel.

After filling his usual green Santa cup, Travis takes a

stool at the bar and begins eyeing my project. He squints. "What is that supposed to be?"

"A gingerbread house," I answer without looking up from my task.

In my peripheral vision, he squints harder. "After a tornado?"

I toss him a sideways glance, then explain, "I've been invited to a little Christmas soirée at the bakery this evening, a gingerbread party. Every business on Main Street is invited to build a gingerbread house to be entered in a friendly contest."

"That sounds horrible," he says.

I ignore that, still focused on the problem at hand. "It's my first year, and I was looking forward to it—but I'm not sure I have the knack for this."

Standing back up, he walks closer and inspects my gingerbread at length, his gaze skeptical. "Your problem here," he finally says, "is poor workmanship."

I blink, drawing my eyes from the gingerbread up to the man across the counter. "Huh?"

"Your icing is your mortar, but you're not using enough. Look at all these gaps." He begins pointing. "Even if you get a roof on it, it's gonna cave in on itself before you ever make it to the bakery. And if this is a contest...well, why aren't you doing something more original than a common house?"

Now I'm the one squinting. Is he serious? "Like?"

Still studying the disastrous pile of gingerbread, he suggests, "How about a gingerbread version of...this building? Your shop."

My jaw drops at the wondrous notion. Only..."That's an amazing idea, but if I can't build a house, what makes you think I can recreate the Christmas Box?"

He gives his head a pointed tilt and reminds me, "Well, you just happen to know someone who's pretty good at building things."

The idea of playing with gingerbread with Travis all day appeals more than I want to admit to myself, or certainly to him. But I still feel obliged to give him an out, in case he just pities me for being so bad at something a child can usually do. "Are you sure you don't mind? I mean, aren't you supposed to be building important things like cabinetry instead of silly things like gingerbread shops?"

"Guess I feel the same way about building things as you feel about Christmas—there's nothing too silly to build. Building stuff is in my blood."

I don't point out that he pretty much just said he got the skill he most cherishes from his father. Nor do I touch on the fact that he's just offered to help me with a full-on Christmas craft. Instead I say, "Well, in that case, I'll take you up on the offer."

By six o'clock, several inches of fresh snow have accumulated on the sidewalk outside, I've had exactly zero customers, and we've built a truly exquisite gingerbread replica of the Christmas Box. With a red-icing ribbon that circles the building, tiny squares of tin foil for windows (on which we've written *The Christmas Box* in red felt-tip pen), and gum drops lining the roof, it's truly a work of confectionary art.

Of course, when I say *we* built it, I mostly mean him. He's a master with the piping bag, and indeed has pieced together a structure so sturdy that perhaps it *could* withstand a tornado. I ran upstairs and made us chicken salad sandwiches for lunch, and I occasionally held a piece of gingerbread while he iced, but mostly I enjoyed watching the artiste at work.

"It's incredible, Travis," I declare as we both step back to take in the finished product.

"Yeah, turned out good," he says easily, his casualness telling me he creates wonderful things all the time and this is just one more. Then he glances outside. "You might be the only entry, though. It's still snowing like crazy out there."

"They're all coming from Main Street," I remind him, "so I suspect they'll still show."

"Well, have fun," he says, reaching for the coat and winter scarf he dropped over a stool hours ago.

Then *I'm* the one peering out the window, reminded that the weather outside is indeed frightful. "Wait," I say as he starts for the door. "What if I drop it?"

He turns to look back. "Huh?"

"I know it's less than a block away, but it suddenly feels like a long hike to the bakery on a snowy sidewalk. Could you help me get it there?"

He flashes a suspicious look, as if he thinks I'm trying to trick him into attending a holiday party. And maybe that's true. But I really *am* worried about dropping his gingerbread masterpiece, too.

"Tell you what," he concedes. "I'll carry it and you hold the doors. But once it's inside, I'm outta there." He hikes a thumb over his shoulder. "Deal?"

I give a short nod. "Deal."

And so after I lace my snowboots and we both wrap up in coats, scarves, hats, and gloves, we set out in the cold for Janie's. We stick close to the buildings, using awnings as partial protection where they exist. At the end of the block, we tromp through slushy snow to cross the street and reach the bakery.

It's cheery and bright inside, already filled with friends and fellow shop-owners I'm looking forward to socializing with. A Christmas tree glows in the front window and a live wreath hangs on the door. When I hold the door open and Travis steps inside, the greetings begin.

"Well, as I live and breathe, is that Travis Hutchins?" asks Andrea Pike, Janie's mother, who must have known Travis as a boy.

"Hey Travis, what's up?" comes from Dara, who then introduces him to her mother, Judy. I'm impressed Dara rolled her here in the wheelchair, but I know Judy was excited about the outing, so I guess Dara refused to let a few inches of snow stop her.

"Well, hello there, Travis," says Helen. "Didn't expect to see *you* here."

"Neither did I," he answers, "but I got tapped for delivery duty." He lowers the gingerbread shop to the long table where other sweet creations reside, then turns to go. "You ladies have fun now."

"You don't think you're actually allowed to leave," says Mrs. Burch, literally rolling her chair into his path.

And before he can even open his mouth to answer, Mrs. Pike adds, "Of course he's not. The more the merrier and I want to hear what you've been up to since you left." She hooks her arm through his. "Come on over to the refreshment table."

As he's led away, I say hello to always-energetic Janie, her sandy hair up in a messy bun as usual, and hold the door open for another gingerbread entry being carried in by Gail from Winterburger.

After which a gasp is let out, and I turn to look as Helen declares, "Oh my. I'm so glad I decided to walk over after getting off work or I'd have missed this glorious sensation of sugar!" She's looking at my entry, of course. Or *our* entry. Well, okay, Travis's entry. "This is brilliant!"

"Lexi, you did *not* make that," Dara announces loud enough for a few of the other party-goers to hear.

Great. My buddy betrays me. "How do *you* know what I made and what I didn't?"

"Because I've seen you decorate cookies. You're good at the rolling and the cutting and the baking, but the decorating is...well, not your forte."

I let my eyes go wide. "Um, wow, traitor much?"

Though she just laughs. "I'm sorry, but you know it's true. And really, it's not that you're so *bad* with icing—it's just that this is so *good*."

"Fine, fine," I confess when I realize everyone is looking at me. "I tried to make it myself, but when it wasn't going very well, Travis leaped in to help and a piece of cookie art was born. It's still the official entry from the Christmas Box, though."

"Well, don't anybody touch it," says Jim from the Winterberry Gazette, pulling out his phone. "I need to get some pictures for the paper."

"Just be sure to put Travis's name on it, even if it *is* from the Christmas Box," Carl from the Country Creamery insists. The middle-aged man looks down over his glasses as he speaks, reminding me that he's a no-nonsense stickler about everything, even gingerbread contests.

"Um, that's really not necessary," Travis is quick to interject. I'm pretty sure tough guy Travis Hutchins doesn't want it advertised that he's been playing with gingerbread.

"No," Janie insists, "fair is fair. The people of Winterberry deserve the truth."

He doesn't argue, probably already realizing it's a lost cause. And when our eyes meet across the bakery, he mouths: *I'm going to kill you.* But I just smile. Because he's cute. And I don't really think he's going to kill me. In fact, I almost think he's starting to like me back.

Not that it matters. He's made it extremely clear that his time in Winterberry is temporary. And we're still just as much opposites today as when I opened my shop a couple of weeks ago, or as we were back in high school for that matter.

But for now...I'll just enjoy his company. Turns out, once I worked my way to letting bygones be bygones, that he was right—he's not such a bad guy anymore.

As people socialize over snacks, my first thought is to go rescue him from whoever's got him cornered, but he looks perfectly comfortable talking to Jordan from the pizza place, and then Dara and her mom. So I leave him on his own and chat with other people—everyone is buzzing about all the snow, whether their shopping is done, and the Winterberry Christmas Festival coming up this Friday night. I find out Janie will be there selling cookies and add that I'll be running the hot chocolate stand. "With her trusty sidekick, me," Dara comes sliding up at just that moment to add.

After refreshments, Janie announces it's time to vote. We all circle the long table set up in the middle of the bakery for the contest and a secret casting of ballots commences. In addition to entries from Winterburger, Thoroughbred Pizza, the Country Creamery, and Janie's, I see gingerbread creations from Kentucky Korner, Uptown Vintage, the Winterberry Antique Mall, the Winterglow boutique, the Cutting Crew Hair Salon, and the Bank of Winterberry. Some of the gingerbread houses are quite elaborate, including one designed to look like a Swiss chalet and another possessing a large, detailed lawn, complete with fondant pine trees and a candy cane fence.

But when Janie counts the votes from the Santa hat she passed around, the resounding winner is the one that looks like my lovely little Christmas shop.

"And so our grand prize—a fifty-dollar gift card for the

bakery—goes to...Travis," she announces, holding it out to him with a smile. Then she looks to me. "Sorry, Lexi, but maybe he'll share with you." She ends on a wink and a laugh.

I'm perfectly happy with the outcome, though. *Don't look now, Travis, but you just went to a Christmas party, with a Christmas craft you created in a Christmas shop today, and you don't even look miserable.* As far as Operation Wish Upon a Star goes, today feels—however unexpectedly—like a big step in the right direction.

Travis

The first thing I do after collecting my gift card? Say my goodbyes and get the hell out of there.

But while trudging back up the street through the deepening snow, I see that, to my surprise, the lights are still on at Winterburger. All I've had since lunch is a cookie and a cup of punch at the bakery, so I don't hesitate to duck in from the cold.

"Travis." The deep, cheerful voice comes from the kitchen—it's the owner and cook, a guy named Nick, who spotted me through the window behind the counter.

I lift my hand in a wave. "Thought you guys might be closed in this weather."

He shrugs. "Got a few customers due to the bakery party, so we stayed open."

I guess the men I see sitting at tables nibbling on fries must have driven their wives to the event.

"Here by myself, though," Nick says, stepping up front

to the register, "so what can I get you? Couple of burgers and fries?"

"Just one tonight," I tell him, then add a soft drink. He probably thinks I'm skipping the manor this evening due to the snow, and that's fine with me. I'm not sure why I assume he knows my business, but the small town grapevine usually keeps up on such things.

Ten minutes later, I'm sitting in a booth enjoying a burger, happy to be by myself for the first time since I crossed the street for coffee this morning. I never expected to end up building a gingerbread shop or going to a party. But maybe the *most* surprising part is: It wasn't awful. And hanging out with Lexi was...well, not a bad way to spend a snowy day. Even if I probably should have been working if I want to get the soap shop done any time soon.

In a way, it reminded me of snow days as a kid—the kind when my friend, Dakota, who lived up the road, would walk down and play board games with me, or we'd put together a big puzzle on the kitchen table. I can still smell the warm chocolate chip cookies my mom would bake for us. There was something nice about having nothing to do but watch the snow fall from a spot where I felt safe and comfortable.

And maybe that's what I needed after yesterday's nursing home visit. Something that felt safe and comfortable and easy. Well, maybe it's not *easy* when she's beating me over the head with Christmas cheer or pressuring me to adopt a dog or sneaking trees in to my apartment. So *easy* is the wrong word. Maybe what I feel when I'm with her isn't that simple to define. All I know is that for some reason, no matter what ridiculousness the woman throws at me, I keep going back for more.

"Well, hello there."

I look up from my burger to see that Helen has wandered down from the bakery.

"Hi, Helen. Care to join?" I motion to the cushioned seat across from me.

"Thanks, but I'm grabbing mine to go. It's been a fun little gathering, but I'm ready to get home to my cats and my Christmas tree." And with that, she makes her way to the counter to give Nick her order.

While she's waiting, though, she comes back to my table, reaching down to touch my shoulder. "It's none of my business, Travis, but...I noticed you weren't at the manor today."

Something inside me stiffens as the last bite of my burger turns tasteless in my mouth. It's the first time I've ever felt anything but affection and appreciation for the woman standing beside me. "Took the day off," I tell her shortly, wiping a napkin across my face.

"Listen, I know what happened yesterday shook you, and I understand. It's hard, what he's going through. But he was back to his normal self today, just so you know."

I nod, thinking things through. I guess I've gotten to know Helen well enough, even if just by accident, that I don't mind being honest with her. "Yeah, it shook me. But it also...brought back some bad memories."

Her brow knits. "I'm sorry to hear that."

"Did he notice?" I ask. "That I didn't come?"

She nods. "He asked if I'd heard from you."

I didn't expect to feel bad about anything while I was here, but suddenly I do. Even though I haven't done anything wrong. I've been trying pretty hard, in fact, to do everything right. Just in case I was wrong *before*— staying away all those years. "Sorry, Helen," I murmur.

"Nothing to apologize for, Travis," she tells me. "You're doing the best you can with this, I know. It's a lot."

"I'll be back tomorrow."

This time her nod comes with a gentle smile. "He'll be glad to see you."

"In the meantime," I say, pushing to my feet, "I gotta get home. I took in a stray dog and she's doing better with her puppy pad training, but it's anybody's guess what I'm gonna find when I walk in the door."

"Aw, kind of you to take her in, poor thing. I'll have to come meet her." Then she gives her head a thoughtful tilt. "Sometimes your dad talks about a dog *he* used to have."

"Blinker," I say.

"That's right," she replies with a sad sort of smile. "A lot of the residents miss their pets, even when it's been a long time."

Damn. I came back to Winterberry feeling—if I'm honest with myself—kind of dead inside. Or maybe that's how I *made* myself feel in order to deal with being home. But lately I can't seem to outrun my emotions, and right now the idea of all these people missing their dogs and cats rips into me deep.

"Burger's ready, Helen," Nick calls and she starts

toward the counter—yet now I'm the one touching *her* shoulder.

"Listen," I say, "I don't know if this is a crazy idea, but..." In fact, it's only half-formed in my head.

"But what?"

Then I tell her what's on my mind.

December 11

Travis

As I traverse slushy roads, some still snow-covered, to Bluegrass Manor, I glance over to the dog in my passenger seat. Part of me can't believe I asked Helen if I could bring Marley to the home. I was even more shocked when she excitedly said, "Oh yes! Please do. We encourage visits by pets—on leashes, of course—but we haven't had any in a long time. It makes the residents so happy—they'll love it!"

Now I just hope Marley doesn't pee on the floor. "*Please* don't pee on the floor," I tell her now.

Though maybe I shouldn't worry—when I got home last night, to my shock, she'd used the pad! On her own! I gave her a treat—even though I think the idea is to do it right when she goes, so she understands why she's getting it.

"You're really moving up in the world," I tell her as we turn into the parking lot. "Just last week you were homeless. Now you're, like, a therapy dog." After putting the truck in park, I take her furry little face between my hands. "Do me proud, girl. Be nice to all the sweet people."

She does surprisingly well on a leash, and now she trots ahead of me like a pro toward the front doors, where I stop to punch in the code that opens them.

As Marley and I step inside, the response is instant. A lost-looking woman in a long, quilted robe bends down to pet the dog, her eyes wide. A man rolls his wheelchair up to get in on the action, saying, "Nice doggie, nice doggie," as he strokes his hand through her fur. Nurse Gabbi comes rushing up, as well, mooning at the pup from behind her black-framed glasses as she reaches down to scratch behind the dog's ears. And Marley's eating up all the attention, licking hands and fingers while her tail goes a million miles an hour.

As I walk her a little farther down the hall, I come upon maintenance and administrative people busy stringing lights and hanging boughs of greenery. Sparkly snowmen made of felt now decorate some of the doors.

"Oh, look at this sweet puppy." I look up to see Helen exit the room to my right and her eyes meet mine. "I'm so glad you brought her—look at how much love she's getting already." Then she stoops to pet the dog herself. "Hello, Marley—it's so very nice to make your acquaintance. Thank you for coming to see us today."

"Looks like you guys are pretty busy here," I tell her

when she raises back up. I motion to the decorating taking place. "Are you sure this is a good day for Marley to make it busier?"

She waves a hand down through the air. "Oh, absolutely. Any day is a good day for a furry visitor." Then she pushes out a big sigh while studying a pile of open boxes filled with holiday stuff. "We're so behind on this. We've been shorthanded too long. Finally, today, I said, 'Just start putting it out.' If we don't, Christmas will come without our residents getting to enjoy it."

That's when she hands me a green wreath dotted with holly berries and takes the leash. "Trade you," she says, then points. "Up on that hook please. It's too high for me to reach."

I do as I'm told, after which she hands me more fake greenery, indicating it should be draped from other temporary hooks already lining the corridor.

"What a help you are!" she says before switching her focus in another direction. "Shannon, come meet Travis's dog."

I glance back to see Shannon roll up in her usual fleece pants, today's sporting multi-colored snowflakes, and like everyone else, she looks delighted at the sight of Marley. She bends to pet her, cooing to her in words I can't understand.

Next thing I know, even Dottie and her babydoll are inching closer, and the old woman is wearing the first hint of a smile I've ever seen on her expressive face.

"Her name's Marley," I tell Dottie from where I'm hanging yet another wreath.

"Mar-ley," she repeats slowly. It's the only time I've ever heard her speak. When Helen raises her gaze to me and our eyes connect, I suspect it's a fairly rare occurrence.

"That's right," Helen tells her. "Marley. Want to come pet her? She's very gentle."

I pause my decorating work, watching as Dottie leans cautiously closer, finally lowering her wrinkled hand to the fur on Marley's back. As if she senses the need for calm, Marley stands extremely still. I'm suddenly very impressed with my new dog's behavior.

More residents come from their rooms to see her as Helen keeps me lining the hallway with boughs of holly and strands of sparkly garland. "I was about to break out a step stool before you showed up," she tells me. "I hope you don't mind me putting you to work."

"Nope," I tell her. I may not like Christmas, but I can instinctively understand the need for cheer here, *any* kind of cheer. If anything about Christmas lights or holly brings the residents any joy, it's well worth dragging it out and hanging it up.

"We always get a live tree," she goes on to say, still holding Marley's leash as an old man behind a walker stoops to pet her, "but every time we've even thought about it so far, it comes a snow and sidetracks Glen, our mainte-nance man, from getting it for us. So that's got to happen after the rest of this is done."

When I turn to ask her, "What next?" she just laughs.

"Take a break," she says." You've saved me a lot of climbing." Then she puts the leash back in my hand. "Why don't you take this little cutie in to see your dad?"

"He's still...?"

She nods pleasantly. "His usual self. I'll even head in with you."

Together, we start toward his room, and she steps in first. "Look who's here, Tom."

"Is it Travis?"

I enter the room as she says, "Not only Travis, but he brought his dog, Marley, to visit."

When Dad's eyes light up, I'm not sure if it's for me or the dog, but it doesn't really matter—it warms my heart to see him smile, to see him being the man I've come to know these last couple of weeks.

"Sorry I didn't make it in yesterday, Dad."

He's shaking his head. "Don't matter—you're here now. And what a cute pup ya got there."

Since Dad is in bed, as usual, I heft Marley into my arms so he can pet her. Like everyone else here, he's fawning over her like crazy, and she's licking at him excitedly. "What a sweetie," he keeps saying. "What. A. Sweetie."

I spend a couple hours going back and forth between walking Marley around the manor and hanging out with Dad.

It's as I'm telling him I need to get back to town and put some hours in on the soap shop, but that I'll bring him his usual burger tomorrow, that he asks me to take some pictures of the work I'm doing so he can see it. I've shown him photos of some of my other custom jobs and he's been impressed.

"Never would've become a carpenter without you teaching me when I was a kid," I admit to him.

That's when I watch a sense of pride come over him that I've never witnessed before. "We had some nice times out in the woodshop back then, didn't we?"

I think of the sailboat. And a hundred other projects, a hundred other moments—all things long put out of my mind until recently. "We did," I agree.

Behind us in the doorway, I hear Gabbi talking with Helen. "I have to work Friday night, so I'll miss it."

"That's a shame," Helen replies.

I have no idea what they're talking about—and neither does Dad, because he asks in a teasing tone, "Whatcha gonna miss just to hang out here with *me*?"

"Christmas Fest," Gabbi says, stepping in to the room. "You going, Travis?"

"Oh, I doubt it," I say. I heard the ladies at the gingerbread bash talking about it, too, some big to-do at the park next to the Christmas Box, but... "Not really my kinda thing."

"Oh, you oughta go," Dad insists. "It's real nice. Whole town comes out."

I'm thrown to hear this since I wouldn't have guessed it was his idea of a good time, either, but he's just full of surprises lately.

"I don't know," I murmur, giving my head a light shake.

"Goodness knows I'd go if *I* was able," he says.

Which is when Helen pipes up, suggesting, "You should take him, Travis."

I turn to her, surprised, my interest freshly piqued. "I can do that?"

"Sure," she answers. "People are more than welcome to take their loved ones on outings. It's nice for anyone here to get a change of scenery—does wonders. You can fold up his wheelchair and put it in the bed of your truck, easy as pie."

It's still not my idea of fun, but I can't imagine what it's like being stuck here day in and day out. Even if Dad hasn't been here long, it probably *feels* long. And he doesn't have much time left, so if he wants to go, I should take him.

"Would you like that?" I ask. "A night on the town in Winterberry?"

"You don't think it'd be too hard to cart me around?" Suddenly, he's Mr. Considerate-Of-Others.

I shrug. "I'm sure we can manage it together if you want to go."

The words put a big smile on his face. "That'd be real nice, Trav."

And as if on cue, Marley lets out a bark. "Sounds like she thinks it's a good idea, too," I say, "so it's a date."

Lexi

I haven't seen Travis all day. He didn't even come in for coffee this morning, and I can't deny that I missed getting to smile into those breathtaking brown eyes. Yeah, breathtaking. That's how I think of them now. I've given up fighting it, I suppose, whatever *it* may be. Attraction. But also more. Though it's still fruitless to think about that since he'll only be here a short time.

Later, I saw him through the window, working in the storefront, and I forced myself not to stare lest he catch me at it.

I had a few customers, but it was another slow day—just too much snow, I guess.

Now I'm curled up on the couch after dark, Crinkle Bear at my side, getting ready to watch "Jingle All the Way", one of my mom's favorite silly Christmas movies. Outside, it's snowing once again, and this time I'm not even surprised.

Reaching over, I pull Crinkle to me, remembering when my grandma gave him to me after my father's November funeral. I couldn't have dreamed she and Mom would be gone, too, before I even turned twenty-one.

What if I can't make a go of the shop and this was all for nothing? Sure, I'd survive. But if it crashes and burns, along with my mom's dreams, I'll feel like I have nothing. Nothing to show for my life but an old building in an old town, and not even anyone to hug but a teddy bear.

I glance over at my favorite photo of Mom and Grandma. They're standing in the diner, wearing Santa hats and silly Christmas aprons. I took it when I came home from college on Christmas break the winter before the fire. "I really miss you guys," I whisper to the photo. "And I want to make you proud. I want to keep the things you loved alive."

But then I set Crinkle aside and start the movie. Because I learned long ago not to get mired in the sadness—I can let myself feel it, but then I have to move through it.

A little while later, Arnold Schwarzenegger has just

outrun an angry reindeer and kicked a wooden wiseman's on-fire head through a picture window when something draws my gaze out my *own* window.

And I gasp at what I see.

The Christmas tree lights in Travis's apartment have just come on.

December 12

Lexi

The next morning Helen comes into the Christmas Box on her day off to shop. And, of course, to chat. We've barely seen each other lately—it being such a busy time of year and me now tied to the shop much of the time—but ever since Mom and Grandma died, Helen's kept in close touch and tried to fill that void.

After a bit of catching up, I ring out her purchases, and she's walking out the door when I hear her issue a merry greeting. "Well, good morning, Mr. Hutchins." Unless Travis's father has somehow gotten himself sprung from Bluegrass Manor, my neighbor across the street is on his way in.

And then there he is, all six handsome feet of him, making my heart beat a little faster at the mere sight.

"I just heard from Helen that you were at the manor yesterday," I can't help saying with a knowing smile.

"That's not exactly a newsflash, Lexi," he points out. "I'm there *most* days. And good morning to you, too, by the way."

I'm still all bubbly about what Helen told me, though. "And I heard the residents had a Christmas canine visitor, and that she was a hit."

He gives his head a confiding tilt. "Okay, that's a little more newsworthy, I guess. But it had nothing to do with Christmas, so quit acting like it did. She was a very good girl for them, though. And she's still using her puppy pads like a pro, by the way."

"That's awesome," I say. But I haven't quite hit my stride yet. "I also heard you hung Christmas decorations for Helen."

At this, he shoots me an are-you-done-now? look. "Guilty as charged. Because she asked for help. And I'd have to be a pretty horrible guy to say no."

But I'm *not* done yet. "*And* I saw the lights. On your Christmas tree last night."

It's like the star on top of my Christmas tree of accusations, and at this, he finally looks as if he's been caught at something. Did he think I wouldn't notice? Or, well, maybe he assumes I have better things to do than spy on him across the street. And maybe I shouldn't be so quick to fill him in otherwise.

But he breaks through my self-doubt with a playful grin to claim, "They're for the dog. The dog likes them."

I tip my head back and reply just as teasingly, "Ah," aware that my smug success is still showing.

"I came in for coffee, by the way," he informs me. "Not

to get grilled on my every move and how it may or may not relate to an upcoming holiday I still don't like."

I simply smile and reach for his mug. "Whatever you say, Mr. Scrooge."

It would seem that Operation Wish Upon a Star is moving forward as planned.

December 13

Travis

I pick Dad up early before the festival, to make sure I beat the crowd and get a parking spot on Main like usual. Every time I've seen him, he's been in pajamas or a sweatshirt and drawstring pants, so when I find him sitting in a wheelchair in a half-zip pullover and blue jeans, I'm caught off guard.

"Whoa, check you out. Mr. GQ all the sudden." He looks healthier in normal clothes. But I can't deny he's gotten thinner just since I've been in Winterberry, despite all his beloved hamburgers.

He casts me a cocky grin. "I still clean up pretty good, don't I?"

Gabbi enters the room behind me and says, "Hey there, Travis. After I get your dad's coat and gloves on, I'll walk you out and help get him in the truck."

My instinct is to say I'm sure I can handle it—since

she's much smaller than me, downright petite, in fact—but I hold my tongue. I always step out when she or Helen helps him to the bathroom, and I guess I don't really know how that goes, but maybe the fact that he can't maneuver himself at all didn't hit home for me before right now.

I push him out through a wet, snow-plowed parking lot, and when I open the truck's passenger door, Gabbi leans down over Dad and he wordlessly places his arms around her neck. "Here we go," she says, hefting him to his feet. "Now we're gonna turn, Tom." After she positions him near the seat, together they get him up into it.

Closing him inside, the small woman in scrubs and a fleece zip-up asks me, "Think you can manage it?"

"Yeah," I tell her, softly, surely—but I wonder if she can see that I'm a little dumbfounded. He's weaker than I realized. And she's stronger, both in ways you can see and ways you can't.

She shows me how to fold up the wheelchair and says, "You two have fun."

The decision to go early was a good one because there are only a few spaces left when we arrive. The closest is marked handicapped, and despite not having one of those official things hanging from my mirror, I take it. Normally I would never do that, but if my father doesn't qualify as handicapped, who does?

"Well, will you just look at all the people," Dad declares, pointing out the window. "And that tree! Sure is pretty. Whole street is, in fact."

Until this moment, I never really noticed how all the storefront windows are lined with colored lights, or took in the pine boughs wrapped around the streetlamps. Glimpsing it through the eyes of a man who hasn't left his nursing home in weeks, a man about to have his last Christmas on this earth, I can see the beauty in the bright, twinkling lights in a way I couldn't have only an hour ago.

After I get the wheelchair from the truck bed, I open his door and ask, "You ready?"

"More than!"

He thinks I'm talking about the festival, but I meant ready for us to maneuver him into the chair.

Turning toward me, he doesn't hesitate to loop his arms around my neck, same as he did with Gabbi. Then I lean in and grip his shockingly-skinny hips as he slides gently from the seat to a standing position on the sidewalk. It's the closest we've been, physically or otherwise, since I was a kid. It's almost like we're slow-dancing. He smells like Irish Spring and the coffee he probably drank with dinner. He's lighter than I even expected. And it's all very awkward for me, but the fact that he's clearly gotten used to such help and takes it in stride makes it easier. Lowering him into the chair feels strange, backward—the parent becomes the child.

What I didn't factor in when taking the spot directly across the street from the park was that I'd have to wheel him down to a corner for handicap access. Suddenly I have profound admiration for caregivers and handicapped people who have to work so much harder to do the things most us take for granted.

As I wheel him toward the nearest crosswalk, past the Lucas Building—where I left a light on in back—he glances through the plate glass window. "Say, why don't you take me in there, let me get a look at your work."

I've forgotten to snap the pictures he asked for, and wheeling him into his brother's old place seems easy enough. I pull my keys from my pocket and, though it takes a little finagling with the chair, I get him inside and flip on the lights.

"Still early in the project," I tell him, then start pointing and explaining. "Both walls will be lined with cabinetry and shelves from front to back when I'm done."

He begins examining some cabinet doors I've just finished, laid across two sawhorses. "Damn fine workmanship," he says, running his index finger along one edge. "Gonna be real nice, I can tell."

He sounds proud, like any normal father might, and despite thinking I didn't care about that, it makes me feel good inside.

I almost say I'll bring him back to see it when it's done, but then I think better of it. It'll probably be only another few weeks, but what if he's too frail by then?

"Ready for the festival?" I ask a little while later.

"Sure thing. But I'm glad we stopped here."

"Me, too." Then, thinking about how much he enjoyed the Main Street lights, I tell him, "Wait right here—I need to run upstairs for a sec."

Heading up, I pet the dog—who I finally remembered to leave a dim lamp on for before I left—and then I walk over and plug in the tree lights.

By the time Dad and I near the park entrance, busy with people moving this way and that, their talk and laughter echoing, lights glowing and holiday music playing, I begin to experience an old, familiar sensation, something in my chest expanding as we grow closer. It's...anticipation.

It's what I felt as a kid walking into an amusement park or even just the county fair. I have no idea where it sprung from—maybe I'm still seeing it all through my father's eyes. But whereas during that tree-lighting party I wanted to stay as far away as possible, right now I'm surprisingly okay with being in the middle of it all.

"Well, hey there, Tom—how ya doing?" asks a man I don't know. I stop pushing so Dad can say hello.

Which is when a woman I vaguely recognize from my childhood but can't place greets him with, "Tom! It's good to see you out and about."

"You both remember my boy, Travis," Dad says, his voice brimming with pride.

Each of them tells me who they are, and I pretend to remember as Dad goes on. "He was nice enough to bust me out of the manor tonight so I could kick up my heels a little." He laughs at his own joke and the rest of us do, too.

We don't make it much farther before more people are greeting Dad, asking him how he's feeling, saying all the right things. It's kind of like taking Marley into a rest home —you've just started moving forward again when someone else stops you. But this is why we came and it's fine with me.

While Dad chats, I find myself scanning the park for Lexi, since I'm sure she's here somewhere. I see Santa Claus with a little kid on his knee in the gazebo, and Janie from the bakery selling fancy, iced cookies, and families posing for pictures in front of the big Christmas tree—but no Lexi Hargrove.

After Dad finishes a conversation with someone and informs me, "I built a deck for that fella a few years back," a teenage girl in an elf costume appears before us wearing a big smile.

"Happy Holidays! Come over by the tree and I'll take your picture."

I start to object, out of the sheer habit of not wanting to commemorate our broken relationship, but when Dad looks up hopefully, I say, "Sure," and push the chair in that direction.

The elf takes my phone and snaps a few shots of us, my hand on his shoulder.

When that's done, I ask Dad if he wants a cookie and wheel him over to Janie's table near the gazebo. He selects one shaped like a mitten. And as he talks with still more friends I never knew he had, I step back to lean against one of the gazebo's thick white posts.

"Pssst," I think I hear someone say nearby, but I ignore it.

A few seconds later, though, there it is again. "Pssst. Pssst, little boy." Now it comes with a weirdly deep voice. "Little boy, come tell Santa what you want."

I turn my head to see that Santa, sitting a few feet away in a big chair, is indeed talking to *me*. He's smiling at me, in fact, and it's getting fairly creepy—until he reaches up to pull down his beard, revealing a familiar face underneath.

"It's just me, Travis." Helen's bold grin tells me she's extremely amused with herself.

I give her a small ya-got-me smile in return. I suppose I shouldn't be surprised—Helen always seems to be at the center of all things Winterberry. But I keep my voice low as I reply, "There's nothing I want for Christmas, Helen."

"But there's something I want *for* you." She sounds mysterious as she reverts to her deep Santa voice, the fake white beard back in place.

"What's that?" I indulge her to ask.

"It's a secret."

I only shake my head and arch an eyebrow in her direction. "Have you been dipping into the eggnog, Santa?"

At this, she just laughs. Then she glances across the park in a way that makes me follow her eyes, until my gaze falls on none other than the person I've been looking for: my pretty neighbor from the Christmas Box.

Ah, I knew she'd never miss a Winterberry Christmas event—heck, she probably *created* the event. She's manning the hot chocolate table, currently helping a little kid spoon chocolate chips on top of a whipped cream-covered paper cup as she wiggles her hips to Kelly Clarkson's *Underneath the Tree*.

Watching from a distance, it's hard to miss what a vibrant woman she is. And a resilient one, too. Some people who've suffered losses—like me— go through their existences angry and bitter. While Lexi somehow still manages to soak up all of life's little joys every single day.

That's when I realize Helen is eyeing me, waiting for some kind of response. I simply say, "Santa, I have no idea what you're talking about. And I have to go push a man around in a wheelchair now."

"You're a good egg, Travis Hutchins," she calls softly behind me, back in her normal voice.

I toss her a wink as I start toward Dad. "Don't let it get around."

A few seconds later, Dad is filling me in on the guys he was just talking to, and saying he heard someone is selling some tasty pumpkin pie over by the cocoa booth.

"You want a slice?" I ask.

"That sounds real good. In fact, think I'll save my cookie for later and eat some pie right now. I'm not real hungry, but I've always loved pumpkin pie."

"I remember," I tell him.

I have no idea if Lexi sees me as Dad and I approach the booth next to hers. But *I* stay very aware of *her*. She's wearing a white puffy vest over a fuzzy red sweater, her long hair falling in gentle waves from beneath a red knit hat with a fluffy ball on top, and now Dara is at her side sporting her usual antlers as both sing along with Kelly.

As Dad digs into his pie a minute later, she catches me looking—so since eye contact has been made, I roll Dad over to her table. "If it's not Mrs. Claus herself," I say with a smile.

"Mr. Scrooge," she greets me. "Behaving less Scroogier tonight than usual, though."

I ignore the teasing accusation in her voice, instead asking, "Do you know my father, Tom? Dad, this is Lexi Hargrove."

"Yes," she says, "we've met here and there along the way. How are you tonight, Mr. Hutchins?" She holds her hand out to him across the table.

He lowers his fork to the paper pie plate to briefly squeeze her mitten-covered fingers in his. "Doing pretty good, thanks. Sure am enjoying this evening. I knew your grandmother from the diner." Then he takes another bite and asks her, "Have you tried this pumpkin pie? Mmm, mmm, mmm."

"Not yet," she tells him.

"You do like pumpkin pie, don't you?" he teases her.

"Do I like pumpkin pie?" she jokes back. "Do reindeers fly? Does Santa say ho ho ho?"

I can't help thinking that the only Santa *I* know doesn't seem to go ho ho ho as much as she tries to play holiday matchmaker. As if I need Helen to point out how cute Lexi is. As if she isn't already on my mind enough without that. As if I don't find myself flirting with her without meaning to. As if every time we touch in some tiny way doesn't make my skin tingle and my chest tighten. Somehow, she's even cuter tonight than usual—a complication I don't need right now. But a question lingers in the back of my mind: How long can I ignore all that?

When yet another friend of Dad's walks up, pulling him into the next conversation, Lexi says to me, "Sweet of you to bring him."

"He wanted to come," I inform her. "Wasn't my idea."

But she just shrugs. "Well, it's still nice. He looks happy. Even if I'm sure you hate this."

I want to say that I do—a knee-jerk reaction. At this point, I kind of have a reputation to uphold. But as I look around at the laughing kids, a snowman someone built near the gazebo, and the tree—its lights sparkling, its boughs glistening with snow—I can't quite do it. So instead, I'm honest. "It's not awful."

Lexi

A little while later, after Travis has waved goodbye and wheeled his father away, a tap comes on my shoulder and I turn to see Brenda, a friend of my mother's who waited tables at the diner back in the day. Her long, silver hair is pulled up into a high ponytail atop her head, a sprig of holly tucked in as an accoutrement. "Who *was* that man, Lexi?" she asks, sounding all dreamy and suspicious.

"What man?" I blink, playing dumb.

Beside me, Dara has tuned in to the conversation, too.

"The very handsome one who sent you this," Brenda replies, holding out a paper plate on which rests a perfect triangle of pumpkin pie heaped with fluffy whipped cream.

"He sent me *pie*?" I scrunch up my nose, feeling both smitten and a little confused.

Brenda nods as if I'm keeping some secret from her, but I just take the plate.

"Is this...like when a guy sends a woman a drink in a bar?" Dara suggests, one fingertip to her lips as she ponders it. "Just the small-town version?" Then she addresses Brenda. "Oh, and he's the long-lost Travis Hutchins, who once stood Lexi up at a high school dance and is now rehabbing the Lucas Building, while keeping watch over his father, Tom, who has a terminal illness."

We both just gape at her dramatic yet concise explanation.

"What can I say?" she goes on. "Mom and I like to watch the few daytime soaps still on. Sometimes I view things through that lens. Especially when the shoe fits. And now that I think about it, this one definitely does. All he needs is a little romance with the girl whose heart he once broke to help him through a difficult time."

But at this, I draw the line. "Don't be ridiculous. He did not break my heart."

She casts me a doubtful look.

So I add softly, "He only bruised it a little."

"Well, all I know," Brenda says, "is that he was a looker. I'd eat pumpkin pie—or pig slop, for that matter—with him any day."

As I try the pie—which I can't deny tastes a little sweeter just knowing where it came from—Brenda is drawn away by another customer, leaving Dara to lean close and say privately, "Don't look now, but I think he likes you, too."

"It's just pie," I tell her.

"And gingerbread buildings and...well, who knows what other scrumptious treats are in your future."

Despite my denials, I can't help feeling a little giddy inside—even if it *is* just pie. I love that he brought his father here tonight—although, wow, Tom looks so much thinner than when I last saw him. I love that he made the gingerbread shop for me, and that he took Marley to visit with people who surely needed it. And I love that he plugged his tree lights in *again* tonight.

Only...it's hard to let myself feel happy for long when I remember why he's here. Because how am I going to feel when his time in Winterberry comes to a close and he gets in that truck and goes back to Chicago for good?

No, he didn't break my heart when he let me down at the Christmas Ball—but if I'm not careful, he might soon.

Travis

After I lift Dad back into the truck, collapse his chair, and get behind the wheel, I glance over to see he's leaned his head back against the seat and is about to conk out. He looks much older than his fifty-five years.

"You okay?" I ask. Though I want to call the words back as soon as they leave me, because of course he's not okay—he's dying.

But he takes the question in stride, telling me, "Think maybe I stayed out past my bedtime." He chuckles a little as he says it. It's 8:30 and we've only been gone a couple of hours.

"Well, I'll have you back to the manor in no time."

As we travel in silence, I'm aware of how small he seems next to me, how frail and docile. I felt the skin and bones of him as I got him back in the truck. But what's consuming me at the moment is the awareness that...it's almost over for him. I *feel* him dying.

Odd, because he's been dying the whole time I've been here, yet suddenly I sense it in a new way. I wonder what it feels like to know this outing might be his last, the last time he talks and laughs with friends, the last time he sees a park, watches kids playing, hears the wetness of the road under tires. Or maybe his feebleness swallows all of that right now and is the only thing that matters—maybe his exhaustion overshadows every thought.

If so, I think he's lucky. Because I'm not sure I'd be handling the situation so well. Despite myself, I admire this ability of his I've witnessed—to live fully in the moment.

Back at the manor, we do that same dance to get him in the wheelchair, and it's harder this time because he's drained and even weaker. When his skinny body is fully in my embrace, the weight of him on me, I experience a rush of emotion I have to push down fast. I don't even know what it is—just a heavy sadness I never expected to feel when I got here.

As I push him through the sliding glass doors, I'm glad to see Gabbi not far up the hall. She's spotted us, too, and heads our way with a smile. "How was it? Did you boys get up to no good?"

We laugh and Dad tells her it was a great time, but he's ready for bed.

"It was nice hanging out with you tonight," I say to him unplanned. The truth is, for all the time I've spent here the last couple of weeks, a lot of it has been the two of us watching TV, and he naps a lot—partly because he's dying and partly due to pain medication that makes him drowsy. I'm glad he held up tonight as well as he did.

"You, too." It comes out as a murmur—he's struggling to stay awake.

That's when I remember the mitten-shaped cookie in my pocket—I put it there for safekeeping. I pull it out and say, "Don't forget this."

His eyes open a little wider. "That's right. A snack for later." He takes it from me, looking as pleased as a little kid.

As I turn to go, I hear him call, "Son?"

Son. When was the last time he called me *son*? I don't even know. I look back. "Yeah?"

"Tonight was real nice. Real special. Thank you for that."

I just nod. I'm not good at this stuff. This I-love-you-I-hate-you-but-now-I'm-starting-not-to-hate-you-quite-so-much-anymore stuff. "I'll be back tomorrow."

Neither of us say anything more, but our eyes meet. It's enough.

Then I turn and head back out into the cold.

December 14

Lexi

The next morning, the Christmas Box is pleasantly busy. I handed out ten-percent-off fliers last night, and the festival got people in a merry, shopping mood. And while offering a discount felt a little desperate, with just over ten days until Christmas, I need to get people through the door.

The wishing box continues to entice shoppers, but even with good days, I'm fighting an uphill battle after all the subpar ones due to snow—or...to the fact that maybe this shop was just a bad idea. My stomach churns every time I allow myself to acknowledge that maybe Travis's initial gut reaction was correct. Then I try to ignore it and keep on believing in wishes.

After all, the wish I made on that star seems a little closer to coming true every day. And it took a while to see any evidence of that. So don't I just need to have faith?

During a break without customers, Dara is tidying up ink pens and paper slips and I'm washing some mugs at the sink. From across the room, she casually asks, "Have you put any more wishes in the box since you and I dropped the first ones in?"

I flinch, glancing up. It's never crossed my mind to. "No. Have you?"

She nods.

I don't know why it surprises me, but it does. I know other people have put multiple wishes in, but maybe to me it seemed...what? Greedy? Which I realize now makes no sense. I go around saying wishes are prayers, but I've never thought anyone was limited to just one prayer. I ask, "What did you wish for?"

I'm surprised, though, when she hesitates—we're usually open with each other. "Isn't this sort of like wishing on birthday candles? That if you tell, it won't come true."

I just shrug, back to my mug-washing. "I never thought about it. But maybe you're right—maybe it's better as a thing just between you and the box and God."

A little while later, she lets out a groan and I glance over to see her peering out the window. So I look, too.

Oh, for crying out loud—it's snowing!

It's begun to feel like some sort of never-dissipating snow cloud is hovering over the town of Winterberry, Kentucky at the worst possible time. I used to love Christmastime snow, but now I'm starting to hate it.

"Maybe it'll stop soon," she offers up hopefully.

I only sigh. "If it doesn't, you can knock off early."

An hour later, we've only had one more customer and

the streets are covered. It's not yet two o'clock, but Dara says, "Maybe I'll head out."

I nod. "Yeah, you should go before the sidewalks get any slicker."

After she leaves, the sleighbells tinkling behind her, I let out a sad sigh.

As snow continues falling and John Legend tells me to have myself a merry little Christmas over the speakers, I walk to the wishing box. Glancing down at the forms Dara created, it strikes me as funny that she included a spot for people's names, like maybe God or fate or whoever else grants wishes won't know who wrote it down otherwise. I pick up a pen, deciding I *will* add another one to the box.

Of all the wishes I've made this holiday season, two have stayed on my mind the most: for Travis to find Christmas joy and for my shop to succeed in every way.

I don't want to *re*-wish either of those things—they're already out in the "wish ether" and I have to keep believing they'll come true. The one about Travis is definitely making progress and, in a sense, the other is, too. I added "in every way," and I *do* see the holiday spirit in people's eyes when they drop a slip of paper into this box, or even when they find the perfect gift for someone. There's more than one kind of success. Now I just need the profit part of the wish to kick in.

So what should I wish for now?

Just look in your heart and don't stop to analyze it. The words enter my head like advice from above, so I roll with it and begin to write.

Name: Lexi
My wish: That Travis decides to stay in town, and maybe he even falls in love with me.

My breath catches when I look down at my own words.

Is that really what I want?

Am I in love with Travis Hutchins?

That fast? That easy?

I don't even know him that well.

But I'm also not sure falling in love is so much about how well you know someone as about what makes your heart take flight.

Glancing out the window, through the snow, I see the shop across the street is empty, but the tree in the window above is lit, even in the middle of the afternoon. And I'm painfully aware that at the very thought of him, my breath goes shallow, my chest begins to tingle, and my heart is indeed fluttering somewhere up above me near the ceiling.

I fold the slip and drop it into the wishing box.

Travis

When I walk into the manor the day after the festival, I find Dad sitting up in bed, but slumped over asleep, and on the table beside him rests the mitten cookie, one bite gone.

That's when Gabbi exits his bathroom. "Hi, Travis. I was just tidying up a little in there." Then she glances at Dad. "Somebody's out like a light. He was awake just a minute ago."

I point at the cookie. "Did he try this and not like it?"

She shakes her head. "No, he was just tired. And not very hungry." She scrunches up her nose, hesitating before she says, "He seems to have less appetite the last couple of days."

Is she trying to warn me about something? If so, she needs to be more direct because I don't get it. "What does that mean?"

She shrugs. "Maybe I'm imagining it. Or maybe not. People start eating less toward the end."

"Ah." I tip my head back, trying not to react. A couple of weeks of ago I couldn't stand the man, after all. And now...now I'm not sure *what* I feel. But it's a lot closer to affection than disdain.

While he sleeps, I watch the TV at the foot of his bed. I think how odd it was to walk in here a few weeks ago and find him treating me like we've been buddies all along, like nothing bad ever happened between us and we didn't spend my whole adult life estranged. But he has brain cancer, so maybe it's one more thing that just isn't gonna make logical sense to me.

And I suppose there are things I wish he'd say, like acknowledging that he wasn't always a good dad, maybe even apologizing for being such a bad one that I left as soon as I could. Unless maybe I'm supposed to just somehow hear that in the kindness he shows me now—maybe I'm supposed to read between the lines? Or maybe that kind of logic, too, is lost in the mist of a brain that's being rapidly eaten by disease.

"You watching 'It's a Wonderful Life' without me?"

I switch my gaze from the TV to the man in the bed. "What?" It was our favorite old movie as a family when I was a kid—we watched it together every Christmas. But that's not what's on right now.

"'It's a Wonderful Life'," he repeats. "You should have woke me for it."

"Dad, this is a Clint Eastwood movie," I inform him.

At this, he manages to look both disappointed and relieved at once. "Well, see if you can find out when it's on. We'll watch it with your mother like always."

I glance over at him, jarred. Where is he in time right now? Or is he *here* in time, but in a different reality, one where Mom never left? Not sure what to say, I hesitate, then settle on a quiet, "Okay."

That's when he spots the mitten cookie, and for a moment looks confused, or surprised, but then points toward it. "Can you hand me that?"

After I do, he takes another bite. Then he shakes his head, as if clearing out the cobwebs. "There for a second, thought I was somewhere else."

I nod, thankful it was only a second.

"Know what?" he asks more cheerfully. "I'm in the mood for something Christmasy after the festival last night. Why don't you find something Christmasy for us to watch."

Inside, I just laugh, thinking I should get Lexi to come visit him—they could really Christmas it up together. But then I reach for the clicker and start through the choices.

"There," he says a minute later. "The Christmas Chronicles. That's a good one. You like that one?"

"Never seen it," I say. I haven't a Christmas movie since...well, since leaving home at eighteen.

"Settle in," he says. "It's a fun one. Kurt Russell is Santa Claus!"

It's after dark by the time I get home. Town is quiet and the streets are messy—it's been snowing all day and it's still coming down.

The Christmas Box is still open, and I glance over to spot Lexi behind the counter, as well as a mom and daughter who appear to be shopping. I sit in my truck for a minute, trying to see a little better—and am pretty sure I can make out the little girl, maybe around ten, adding a wish to the box I made.

After I head inside, feed the dog, feed myself, and then change the pee pad, I walk to the window and look out, surprised to see Lexi's shop still brightly lit. But it ignites a fire in me.

Reaching for the coat I hung on a wall hook just a little while ago, I glance to Marley, currently curled up under the tree like a furry present. "Sorry to take off again," I tell her, "but I have to deal with something."

Something that's bothering me. About the wishing box. About that little girl I saw from my pickup. It's lingered in the back of my mind since I built the box, but seeing a kid actually drop a wish into it just brought my concern to the forefront.

Crossing the quiet street in workboots that have had to

double as snowboots lately, I wipe my feet on the mat inside the shop's door as the bells announce my arrival.

The place is empty now and Lexi looks up from where she's restocking some serving plates on a table. When she smiles at me, I feel it low in my gut. "Coffee's still hot," she tells me. "Or cocoa, too, if you prefer."

"Actually, some hot chocolate sounds good." I haven't been out in the cold much today, but it still feels that way for some reason. "Was surprised to see the store still open, all things considered."

"Yeah, I know. Mostly, I've spent the afternoon restocking and cleaning—and I read half a book. But I've actually had four customers since the snow started, which is four more than I expected. All people who live within walking distance." She sighs. "I'm pretty sure most people are curled up by their fireplaces, filling their stockings online." She punctuates the thought with a little shiver. I guess online retail *is* the worst fear of a small town shopkeeper. "How was *your* day? Spend it with your father?"

I nod, helping myself to a mug of cocoa. "He slept for a while, and then we watched a couple of Christmas movies."

At this, she stops what she's doing to let her blue eyes widen on me.

"His choice, not mine," I'm quick to point out.

She arches her eyebrows. "A misery for you then, I presume."

I want to say yes. Again, I have a reputation to preserve. But just like last night in the park, I'm honest. "They weren't awful."

In response, she smiles like she knows something I

don't. Like she thinks she's reformed me. So I set her straight. "Don't get all excited. My heart still hasn't growing three sizes like the Grinch's or anything like that. No 'dah-who dor-aze' over here."

Yet at this she casts a smug glance to say, "Hmm. You know the words to the Whos' song."

"I know the words to *lots* of The Who's songs," I inform her teasingly. *My Generation, Pinball Wizard, Magic Bus.*

At this, the trill of her pretty laughter echoes down through me. "My mother and grandmother knew all those songs, too, from like a hundred years ago. Different Whos and you know it."

"Okay, okay," I confess, giving her a grin. "So arrest me and take me to Christmas jail. Or—wait, don't, because that would be the worst torture I can imagine."

She just laughs some more, and so do I.

"And what can I say? I like vintage stuff. Music. Movies. Automobiles." I hike my thumb in the general direction of my truck.

"And Christmas cartoons, apparently," she points out.

I just roll my eyes, but *am* a little embarrassed that I seem to remember everything that ever happened in Whoville. Then I cross the room and peer down at the box I built for her. "So people have kept on putting wishes in here, huh?"

She flashes a proud smile. "If this shop were a sundae, the wishing box would be the cherry on top. People are enchanted by it—just as I knew they would be."

"Well," I say, "I have a big question for you about this box."

She appears intrigued, and still just as merry. "What's your question, Mr. Scrooge?"

"What now?"

She blinks, giving her head a puzzled tilt. "What do you mean?"

"What's gonna happen when no one's wishes come true?"

At this, her face droops a little, telling me this has never crossed her mind. She nibbles her lower lip slightly, then tries to force a smile back into place. "Maybe some of them will?"

"What makes you think so?" I shoot at her. I'm not trying to be difficult—just realistic. I made the box, after all, and maybe I feel some weird level of responsibility now, despite myself.

"Well," she reasons aloud, "if a little girl wished for a Barbie doll for Christmas, she's probably also told her parents and maybe written it in a letter to Santa they've seen. I'm sure most of the kids' wishes are like that—gifts their parents already know they want. And others might come true because…they just do."

"I disagree," I tell her firmly. "I think that box is giving people false hope."

When her expression goes grim, I can see I've poked the bear. "No hope is false," she claims vehemently. "I've told you before—wishes, and hope, are like prayers. .And sometimes prayers are answered."

"But sometimes they aren't."

Now she goes from grim to downright combative, scowling at me. "Yes, if someone wishes for Santa to drop a

Maserati in their driveway on Christmas morning or to be crowned the king of England, those probably aren't gonna come true. But I think most people wish for things that *can* happen and really *might* happen."

I let my brow knit, pondering it myself, but in a different way than her. "First of all, I think people are just as likely to wish for something improbable as they are for things that have a good chance of happening. But my point is...if there are things in that box that *can* happen—if somebody knows about them—then maybe you should see if there are some you can...help along."

She looks like I just dropped a bombshell on her. Her eyes go even wider. "I believe in the power of wishing, but you expect me to personally be some kind of a...wish magician?"

I'm still putting this together in my head, but I tell her, "Look, it's not about being a magician—it's about finding ones you can help with, from a logistical standpoint. And okay, sure, I'll agree that most gift wishes from kids are probably already on their parents' radar. But if somebody's wishing for something 'gettable' that their friends or family probably don't know about—maybe you drop a hint to the right person or something. That's all. Just...do a *little* magic."

She still looks just as puzzled, though. "How do we even *see* the wishes?" she asks like she thinks she's stump me. "How do we get them out of the box, Houdini?"

I just tilt my head. "Lexi, Lexi, Lexi. Do you really think I would built a box without a way to open it?" And with that, I walk over, pick up the box, and carry it to the counter. After which I tell her, "The bottom slides out," and pull the slat from the grooves that hold it in place. "*Voilà!*"

All the wishes of Winterberry drop out in a pile on the bar.

Lexi

At the sight of all those little slips of paper now on the counter, two thoughts hit me at once.

Did I actually think the box couldn't be opened? Why did I never ask him?

And the much worse one: *My* wish is in there! The one about *him*! The one about wanting him to fall in love with me!

Why did Dara have to put that name line in the form? And even if she hadn't, it would be pretty obvious who wrote it. This is my worst nightmare. Getting stood up at the Christmas Ball? Mere child's play. *This* is what true horror and humiliation are made of. My chest tightens and my throat seizes.

"Are you okay? You don't look well."

I'm blinking rapidly—in a panicky way, and having trouble breathing. If I were older, I'd fear I was having a heart attack. "I...feel woozy." It's not a lie.

"Are you ... dehydrated or something? Did you have dinner?"

I blink some more, trying to think through the sickening panic. "I ate, but...I'm kind of nauseous."

I lower myself to a stool by the coffee bar and rest my head in my hands. *Think.*

"Are you coming down with something? Do you need to lie down?"

Breathe. Think and breathe. "Maybe my dinner didn't agree with me." Then an idea blossoms. "You know what I really need right now?"

"What?"

"A Coke, from Winterburger. Would you mind?"

I'm waiting for him to go flying out the door—but instead, he asks, "Do you think they're still open? It's been a long, snowy day—I assumed everyone had shut down early."

"*I* stayed open," I point out. Then I raise my head from my hands just long enough to hold them out, palms up, in a who-can-say? shrug. "All I know is that a Coke always makes me feel better when I'm nauseous."

Finally, he says, "Okay—I'll find you one. Hang tight."

He hadn't taken his coat off, so back out into the snow he goes, my knight in shining armor who I've just lied to. I feel awful, but it was entirely necessary. Once he's headed up the street, I fly to the pile of wishes and start rifling through them like a maniac, in search of my name and handwriting, knowing I don't have much time. *Please, please, please.*

I barely register anything I see that isn't my wish. My heart feels ready to explode in my chest, and my hands tremble as I frantically sort. *Where is it already?*

I'm starting to panic all over again because I'm finding

ones I've already checked, including my own about the Christmas Box—*but where's the one about Travis?*

And then—there it is! Between my fingers. cringe at the words—*maybe he even falls in love with me*—and that's when I hear the sleighbells on the door jingle. My heart nearly stops as I cram the wish into the pocket of the long cardigan sweater I'm wearing. Crisis averted.

I look up to see him carrying a can of soda. "Winterburger was closed, but I had some in my apartment, so I ran up and grabbed one from the fridge."

I really do feel unsteady and sick, so I'm not sorry to see it. "Thank you," I say as he walks up, popping the top. I take it from him, our fingers brushing, and swallow a sip. Then I let out a big sigh. "I'm already doing a little better, but this will help." A *lot* better actually. I feel like I've just gotten away with some kind of a crime—the crime of stupidity, perhaps.

I drink some more Coke, and he warms up with his cocoa, wrapping cold hands around the mug. And when, a few minutes later, I announce my complete recovery, he says, "Then let's look at these wishes and see if there are some you can make happen."

"All right," I agree quietly, mainly still just basking in relief.

He plucks up a slip of paper from the pile I just dug through like a madwoman and reads it to me. "World peace. Okay, we can't do that." Then he sets it aside.

"Fair enough," I say. That's a big one." Then I pick one up. "Marissa Compton—who didn't sign her name but I know it's her—wants her boyfriend, Cash, to propose at Christmas."

He blows out a breath. "Really? No jewelry? No clothes? Everybody went super big?"

But I'm already busy thinking. "I know Cash. His father, Nick, owns Winterburger."

Travis tips his head back. "Oh, yeah, Nick. Nice guy."

"All right," I say, widening my eyes on him, "since it sounds like you're friendly with him, maybe you can find a time to chat Nick up about this. Marissa and Cash are both in their late twenties and have been together for at least five years. And I happen to know Nick and his wife *love* Marissa."

Travis squints at me doubtfully. "So I'm supposed to tell this guy I barely know that he should browbeat his son into proposing?"

I shrug. "It's worth a shot. I know you can find a way to bring it up."

"Um, sure," he says, sounding the exact opposite of sure.

As we keep going, we find other similarly challenging ones. Greg Banks didn't put his last name on the form, but I can tell it's him; he wishes his partner, Michael, would agree that it's time to adopt a baby. "Michael is my UPS delivery guy," I tell Travis. "Next time he's here, I'll figure out a way to...pry into an intensely personal part of his life?"

"Good luck with that," my partner in crime says dryly.

But some get easier. An unsigned one reads: *I wish for a nice gift from my husband on our 25th anniversary on*

Christmas Eve. "That's gotta be from Gina—she's married to Carl from the Country Creamery." I point toward the building next door to the south. "He's a pretty rigid, pragmatic guy—I can believe he'd skip a big anniversary, not thinking it's important. But I can easily drop a hint that won't seem related to this box."

Then I open a wish from Dara and read it aloud. "I wish that my mother can somehow get up to Lexi's apartment for Christmas dinner." And my stomach drops.

"What does that mean exactly?" Travis asks.

I let out a sigh. "Every year since my mom and grandma died, I host Christmas dinner for anyone in town who doesn't have somewhere else to go. It's become a tradition. Helen comes, Dara and her mom, and we have a handful of others—Dean from the post office, who's been alone ever since his wife died, and Elaine Mitts, who's usually by herself because her kids all moved far away and don't come home for the holidays.

"Anyway, until a few months ago, I lived in a cottage half a mile up Main Street, near the big curve, but I sold it as part of opening the shop, and this is the first year dinner will be upstairs here. And..." I stop and shake my head. "...I didn't even think about Judy's wheelchair. I feel like a dolt. And I guess Dara felt bad bringing it up." I release another sigh, then lift my gaze to his. "Maybe I should see if Helen can host—but she takes on more shifts around the holidays so other people can take off, in exchange for not having to work on Christmas Day, so I'd hate to ask her. Or maybe Dara and her mom would prefer having it at their house— but no," I say, thinking out loud. "It's small and cramped, and Dara would love a bigger place for them. They never have people over."

I lift my gaze to his. "And you should come, by the way. I would have invited you sooner, but with you hating Christmas and all, I didn't figure you'd darken my door. Now that you seem to hate it a little less, I hope you will." Then I cringe. "Even if, now, I'm not sure what to do about Dara's mom, which kind of puts an enormous damper on the whole event." No wonder Dara didn't want to tell me what she wished for.

"Look," he says in a calming voice, "let's just think about this for a minute. How wide are the steps to your apartment?"

"Pretty wide," I answer. "I can show you." I lead him into the back room and point to the old wooden stairway.

"She's not a big woman," he says. He's right—in fact, she's thin and petite. "Surely I can get her up to your place, as long as she doesn't mind letting me carry her. Do you think she'd be okay with that?"

"She's pretty easygoing," I tell him, "so yes, totally."

"Then problem solved."

"That means you'll come?" My eyebrows raise slightly.

He tosses me a sideways glance as we stand in the back room near a little wooden desk that holds my business computer. "I feel like I've been tricked," he says. "Into a major Christmas activity."

I only shrug. "Well, you don't *have* to come. But then Judy can't, either. And everyone's holiday is ruined. No pressure, though."

The Christmas Box

He tilts his head, looking irritated and amused at the same time. "Sounds like I'm coming to Christmas dinner."

When we return to the pile of wishes, we find plenty more that we can't help with—people wishing for improved health or relationships—and have to set those aside. "I'm depressed now, though," I announce, "since you've made me feel responsible for granting these."

And he doesn't let me off the hook—exactly. He just says, "Well, all you can do is keep looking for the easier ones."

I continue making a stack of some that feel possible. For instance, though she left her name off, I recognize Mikayla Watkins' wish for a Christmas tree for her little ones because she can't afford it. I hold that one out to show Travis. "Mikayla's having a tough year—her husband left her for another woman and has pretty much just disappeared," I explain. "She brought her kids in just to put wishes in the box, and I gave them all hot chocolate. I can donate a tree."

He gives his head a tilt. "Find all the kids' wishes and maybe those are doable, too?" he suggests.

"Yes, that's a great idea," I tell him—then we move on. There are so many to go through that we can't linger.

A moment later I read aloud from another slip, "Eve Lindley wants a visit from Christmas carolers, like in the old days. She's a nice elderly lady—nearly ninety. What a sweet, simple sort of wish."

"If you know any carolers," he says dryly, as if she's requested the impossible, and sounding more like his old Grinchy self.

"That one is *completely* doable," I declare with fervor. "Easy peasy, in fact." I add it to the pile.

And he opens another. "Someone named Darlene— no last name—wants Christmas cookies because she can't make them anymore and it just doesn't feel like Christmas without them."

I nod. "Darlene McIntosh was famous for her cookies around town—she used to make dozens and dozens and give them to everyone she knew. But she's in her seventies now and has a bad back, so..."

"So it sounds like you're making cookies," he says with a grin.

"You have to help me," I demand. "With all of this."

"I do?" He balks. "Because between Dad and renovating, I'm pretty busy. And you've already got me talking to Nick and carrying Judy up the stairs. Plus, I have a dog now."

I actually can't tell if he's kidding or not, but I flash him a look of warning. "You made me open the box."

Slowly, reluctantly, he concedes with, "All right, all right. Where do we start?" And that's when I realize he was just keeping up his Scrooge routine. As if I haven't already seen all the chinks in his armor.

I smile. "Tomorrow we can bake cookies and collect gifts for Mikayla's kids."

He looks doubtful, though. "Uh, don't you have a shop to run here?"

"I'll see if Dara can come in," I tell him, then get back to planning. "After that, we can make some deliveries. And I'll donate a tree and ornaments to take to Mikayla's.

Maybe we can drop them on her porch with gifts after dark—with a note from Santa—so she won't know where they came from."

He looks a little overwhelmed, dark eyes growing wide. "We're doing this all in one day?"

I just shrug. "Like you said, we both have a lot to do and Christmas is coming fast. So we should accomplish as much as we can as quickly as we can."

"Guess that makes sense. But if I'm playing Santa all day tomorrow—" He pauses, giving a playful shiver of horror at his own words. "—then I'd better head home."

"And I'll get busy making lists for everything we need to do."

After we say goodnight, I stand at the front door and watch him cross the slushy street in the dark. Despite myself, I'm excited. I thought the box was just a wishing box, but now it's also becoming a wish-*granting* box, which goes way beyond my original vision for it, but in a wonderful way. And...well, if it means getting to spend more time with Travis, that makes it even better.

Flipping the lock behind him, I return to the bar and go through the rest of the wishes, finding the ones from Mikayla's three kids, and also pulling out a few more I think we can accomplish. The rest I put back inside and say a prayer for as I carry the box back to its table.

That's when it occurs to me that maybe I should put my own back in the box as well. Or...throw it away in case Travis suddenly decides to go through them again.

I reach in my pocket to retrieve it—only the pocket is empty. It's gone. Whoa.

That can't be, though, so I reach deeper, into the corners.

But no wish.

I keep looking, even turning my pocket inside out—but there's still no slip of paper to be found.

Where could it be?

I carefully retrace my steps back to the bar, looking around table legs and the bottom of the counter. It couldn't have gone far—yet I can't find it anywhere.

Well, the important thing is that it didn't end up in Travis's hands.

And I have a lot of work to do on wishes I *can* have some control over, so I'd best shift my focus there. I already can't wait for tomorrow.

December 15

Lexi

Travis and I worked side by side this morning in my kitchen, baking cookies. He's not much of a baker, but I'm not much of a cookie decorator—as Dara so bluntly informed me—so it worked out.

My favorite moments: when he reached up to brush some flour from my cheek (thank God I'm messy in the kitchen) and when he kept nabbing pinches of cookie dough to eat and I finally had to grab onto his hand to stop him. Did I hold on too long? Did he notice? I'm not sure, but when he teased me, saying, "You know you want some," then popped a bit into my mouth, too, his fingers brushing my lips...well, let's just say it was delicious in more ways than one.

Now I'm packing them up, not only for Darlene McIntosh, but also for my grandma's old friend Mrs. Brewster, a shut-in who wished for some visitors this holiday season, and the Parkers, an elderly couple who wished for "unexpected blessings this holiday season." I'm hoping cookies and good tidings do the trick.

After we deliver them, Travis's trusty, snow-worthy pickup will carry us over slick roads to the Holly Ridge Walmart, where we'll pick up gifts I didn't have at the shop. Since I'm donating a tree, lights, ornaments, a stuffed Rudolph for Mikayla's youngest, and a winter hat with a ball on top to make sure Mikayla gets at least one gift herself, Travis offered to foot the bill for the rest. In fact, he tried to pay *me* for the donations, but I refused.

Even though maybe I should have accepted his generosity given how quickly Christmas is approaching and that it's snowing again today and that even though business picked up after word got out about the wishing box, now it's down again. However, right now I'm on a mission to deliver Christmas cheer and trying to ignore the harsher realities facing me.

The tree and other items bound for Mikayla's, along with a shopping bag full of cookie containers, sit next to the door. "As soon as Dara gets back, we'll go," I tell Travis. She's picking up a late lunch at Thoroughbred Pizza. "First stop, Darlene McIntosh's."

"I just thought of something," he says, sounding glum.

I blink. "What's that?"

"We should have made enough cookies to take some to the manor."

"Ugh, you're right." I sigh, now downcast along with him. "Maybe...tomorrow? Even though I suspect we'll still be busy granting wishes."

The Christmas Box

He holds up one finger. "Wait. I just happen to have a hefty gift card for the bakery burning a hole in my pocket."

"That's right— great idea! Cookies for everyone!" Then, anticipating our departure, I reach in my shopping bag and pluck out a Santa hat. "Here," I say, holding it out to my companion. "For merry deliveries."

He gives me an are-you-serious? look. "No way."

I just roll my eyes. I mean, I know he's got his anti-holiday rep and all, but... "Come on, wear the hat. We're trying to give people happy holidays here, and a Santa hat is always a festive touch."

"Nope," he says, sounding resolute. "That's where I draw the line."

"That's your line?" I ask. "At a hat?"

"Yep."

I hesitate only briefly before saying, "Fine," abandoning the hat on the counter to reach back in the bag. "Antlers it is." I pull out a pair of brown velvet antlers attached to a headband. They're wrapped with red ribbon adorned with small sleighbells. Using both hands, I firmly place them on his head.

"I'm not wearing these," he says staunchly, even while wearing them.

"Well, just so you know," I say, picking up the Santa hat and plopping it on my own head, "they look adorable." But —yipes—did I just tell him *he* looked adorable?

Fortunately, he doesn't seem to notice because he's got bigger fish to fry—or antlers to reject. Yanking them off with one hand, he plucks the hat from my head with the other. "Trade ya," he says, then puts the hat on.

169

I feign astonishment. "I thought a hat was where you drew the line."

He tosses me an annoyed glance. "Suddenly it doesn't seem so terrible."

"That's what I thought," I say with a small, winning smile. Mission accomplished.

Travis

I watch as Lexi moves through the halls of Bluegrass Manor like it's nothing. Like it isn't heart-wrenchingly tragic to see so many people no longer in control of their lives, their health, and in many cases, their minds.

I see her hold out a tree-shaped sugar cookie to the man who took Dottie's doll. He's wearing that same odd little smile as always when she offers up, "Merry Christmas."

He says nothing, just takes the cookie. And maybe I'm imagining this, but something in his expression makes me think it was nice for him to be noticed, acknowledged, given something. I feel like a jerk all over again for yelling at him.

I watch her repeat the gesture again and again, kind of in awe, and maybe I'm beginning to wonder if...that's the point? Of Christmas? People with good hearts like Lexi's making other people feel valued?

"That's my girl there."

I turn to find that Helen has snuck up on me in a pair of gingerbread-man-sprinkled scrubs.

But her eyes are trained on the woman in antlers, offering cookies and smiles to every person in sight—some in robes, others fleece; most seated in wheelchairs that have become all too familiar to me. "Despite how bitter she could be, she keeps on shining her bright light out into the world."

"No wonder you two get along so well," I remark. "You kinda do that, too."

She casts me a coy, playful smile. "Sweet talker."

I just laugh. Then tell her, "I barely recognize you, by the way, without your red coat and beard."

"That was a lot of fun," she says. "Getting to hear what all the kiddos want for Christmas. And getting to enjoy the look on your face when you thought I was a creepy old man." She lets out a laugh so big it echoes.

"Yeah," I say, my voice thick with sarcasm. "Hilarious."

"So you two are out spreading holiday cheer today?"

I keep it simple. "Something like that."

"Well, there are certainly worse ways you could spend your time. And worse people to spend it with." She ends on a wink.

But I'm not going there with her, so I change gears. "How's Dad today?"

Her expression does nothing to reassure me. It reminds me of Gabbi's the other night: one that's learned to accept—and convey—hard realities. "He's in fine enough spirits. But his pain is increasing. We're having to medicate him a little more heavily to keep him comfortable."

I consider asking if this means the end is near, but I hold the question inside. Maybe I don't want to know. "Think I'll go check in on him," I tell her. "Let the light-shining reindeer know where I am when she's done passing out cookies."

Helen nods, and as I walk away, she calls behind me, "Nice hat."

Crap. Forgot I had the damn thing on.

Lexi

After Travis and I do a stealth cookie drop on the McIntosh porch, Marianne Jorgensen surprises me by coming out of the house next door—I didn't realize she was Darlene's neighbor.

"I see what you did there, Lexi Hargrove," she says softly from her porch, wrapping a long cardigan sweater tighter around her to ward off the cold. "Darlene will be thrilled by a secret delivery and I won't breathe a word."

I step over into her yard to say, "It wasn't just me. It was Travis, too." I motion toward the man in the Santa hat already making his way back to his truck, parked on the residential street. "We just want to make sure everyone gets something in their stocking this year."

She flicks her gaze back and forth between me and him several times. "I don't know this Travis guy," she finally says, "but if I were you, I'd be hoping to get *him* in my stocking."

I just laugh, like she's so crazy to suggest such a thing. I don't tell her I'm way ahead of her. Or that, despite my wish, I have no idea if I should even *want* him in my stocking—if he's just going back to his other life in Chicago soon. All I know is that without him, we wouldn't be making these Christmas wishes come true.

It's after dark when we head back to Main Street. While Travis grabs us a couple of to-go pizza slices for an on-the-run dinner before we set out on our last delivery of the day, I pop in to the Country Creamery and buy an ice cream cone I don't really want, in order to chat Carl up.

As he dips my cookies-n-cream, I ask, "Don't you have a big anniversary later this month? What are you getting Gina?" I smile my enthusiasm to let him know it's something worth making a big deal of.

"Indeed we do," he tells me. "Our twenty-fifth. But we don't waste money on things like that." He ends with a short head shake, peering at me over his glasses as usual. I've long thought ice cream is too cheerful a business for a man of Carl's temperament.

"Carl, Carl, Carl," I lecture him. "You really must. A twenty-fifth anniversary is a huge accomplishment. Can you just imagine how loved and appreciated Gina will feel being surprised with a special gift to commemorate twenty-five beautiful years together?"

Passing the finished cone over the high glass counter, he narrows his gaze on me skeptically. "You really think that's necessary? What would I even get?"

"I do. And jewelry," I answer without missing a beat. "A pretty bracelet or necklace. Go to a jeweler. Let them help you pick out the perfect thing. It doesn't have to be pricy. But not too cheap either." I point a finger in his direction, knowing him to be a penny-pincher. Which is fine—

except for those times when it isn't. "I think Gina would find it very meaningful."

As I pay for my unwanted cone, he casts me a sidelong glance, as if wondering what I know and how I know it, but thankfully he doesn't ask. "I'll think about it," he replies instead.

"Don't just think. Buy. It's a special occasion," I remind him, then head back toward the red pickup at the curb, hoping our final delivery goes as well as the rest.

As we drive toward Mikayla's little house on a twisty country road outside town, we're both tired, and quiet, because it's been a long day. But a gratifying one.

I wonder if Travis is quiet because of his dad, too. At the manor earlier, Tom woke up only long enough to seem glad to see us and to nibble on the last cookie in the tin from the bakery. I stood in the doorway, watching from a distance as Travis bent over his father, brushing cookie crumbs away and straightening his blanket, almost tucking him in, the same way I'm sure Tom once tucked Travis in at night years ago.

"There," I tell him now, pointing out the little house. Lights shine inside, but there are no signs that it's Christmas. Travis steers slowly past the gravel driveway, not stopping, and we find a place to park the old Ford a short distance up the road next to a dilapidated barn.

After Travis hoists the five-foot artificial tree over one shoulder and I grab out various shopping bags, the two of us go trundling up the snow-lined road like a couple of wintertime thieves in the night. "Guess you're experienced at this," he whispers.

"At what?" I whisper back.

"Sneaking Christmas trees around under the cover of darkness."

"We snuck yours around in the daylight," I correct him, still doing the loud whisper thing. "When you weren't home. This will be trickier—being quiet as we drop everything off."

That's when I trip over something and go sprawling into the piled-up snow on the roadside with an, "Oomph." Following closely behind, Travis comes tumbling down on top of me, his weight pressing me deeper into the drift, tree branches poking into my neck. He mutters a few curse words, then asks if I'm okay.

"I'll survive," I tell him as he gets to his feet, then reaches down, pulling me up by one mitten. It happened fast, but the warmth of his body on mine pretty much overrode anything else like branches in necks or freezing cold snow.

"We're pretty bad at this so far," he announces.

"But our hearts are in the right place," I remind him. "I just hope the tree's not damaged."

He sets it upright on the road and tries to inspect it in the dark, pulling out his phone to shine it on the branches.

"Stop—they might see," I caution him, reaching to cover the light.

"Oh, right," he says. And I realize we're almost holding hands now, around his phone, and I like it. Even through mittens, it's nice.

"We have to be more careful as we get closer," I warn softly once we're moving again, me with the bags and him with the tree. It takes a lot of quiet creeping for us to push through the sagging wooden gate, but then we follow a beaten-down path over the snow to the wide front porch.

As we step quietly up onto it, lugging all our surprises, I spot a tow-headed pre-school boy I know to be named Caleb near the front window, sitting cross-legged on a rug, watching a TV that's apparently right beside the window. "Get out of sight," I whisper to Travis, realizing we're directly where he could notice us.

We both flatten our backs against the house, side by side. Even in the dark, I can make out that Travis looks a little exasperated, and I'm stressed, too. But a moment later, he props the tree in a corner near the door, and I leave my bags beside it, a card from Santa tucked in one of them. After exchanging satisfied glances, we go scurrying back to the gate, rushing to get away in case our movements bring anyone to the door.

As we walk briskly back up the road, our relief is palpable, and he lets out a low laugh, declaring, "That was weirdly fun."

"It was," I agree with a smile.

"Come on, let's get going," he says, then grabs my hand and pulls me into a jog toward the truck. The cold air suddenly feels exhilarating. Or maybe it's his hand in mine.

Or maybe it's what I know for certain in this moment: That at least one of my wishes has really come true. He might not ever admit it, but I know he's feeling the holiday magic right now, the magic I wished for him. And I am, too.

Or...could it be something else altogether making my heart expand in my chest?

As recently as yesterday I questioned the notion that I might be in love with Travis Hutchins. But today if feels a whole lot closer to being...undeniable.

December 16

Lexi

Late last night I discovered a wish from Carol Ann Vaughn for a wheelchair ramp for her mother, Kathryn, and when Travis comes over for coffee this morning, I explain that Kathryn has become almost housebound. "They have a really hard time getting her in and out now. She has one of those electric chairs with the sturdy wheels on it, and if she could bring it outside, she'd have so much more independence—she could ride it up here to town, or even just be out in her own yard with more ease." I tell him her house is right around the corner, "on Williams Drive, right off of Grant, and I happen to know from chatting with Carol Ann that they have Kathryn out of the house all day for some doctor's appointments in Lexington."

"So what you're suggesting," he says from his usual stool at the end of the bar, green speckled mug in hand, "is that you think I can design, construct, and install a wheelchair ramp *today*, before they get back."

I merely nod, hopefully. "Can you?"

He shrugs. "Probably. Need you to take me there ASAP, though, so I can get some measurements and draw up a plan. No time to lose."

I pull out my phone and call Dara, with fingers crossed. "Any way you could mind the store again today? Travis and I have more wishes to fulfill."

When I explained why I needed her on such short notice yesterday she thought it was awesome, and now she says, "Sure. Give me twenty minutes."

It's not snowing, so I'm hoping for a profitable day at the Christmas Box while I'm gone, but I'm mainly just focused on bringing some good in to the world however I can.

Travis

Part of me can't believe I'm installing a wheelchair ramp I just hammered together in a couple of hours in Dad's workshop out at the farm. That same part of me can't believe how often the word "wheelchair" has come into my conversations these last few weeks. Up to now, I'd never even been around anyone in a wheelchair; they were just a distant thing in other people's lives. But now I've come to understand how much they matter for people who need them to be mobile, so I'm happy to do it.

Lexi stands beside me, passing me tools, and when I'm

done, I climb on top of the ramp and bounce a few times to make sure it's sturdy.

Then I stand back in the snow to take a look. "All done," I say. "And if the time comes that it's no longer needed, it can be removed and the steps underneath will still be intact."

My companion flashes a pretty smile, her eyes looking especially blue in the bright sunlight. "This is so awesome, Travis. I love that they're going to come home and just find it here. They'll be so excited. Christmas magic at its finest."

Taking that in, I can't help but give my head a skeptical tilt as I drop a hammer back in my toolbox. "This isn't magic, Lex. I built it."

She looks unconvinced. "Isn't it, though?" she suggests. "Magic can come in many forms."

But I'm not getting it. "What do you mean?"

She's still smiling that smile I feel in my gut. "Magic can be...unexpected kindness," she said. "Generosity. Good will. Talent. Skills. Magic can be a Grade-A Grinch building a ramp for someone who needs it."

I simply slant her a look and keep arguing. "I still say none of those things are magic."

"Maybe magic is like beauty then," she argues back. "In the eye of the beholder."

When we hear kids laughing from somewhere behind the modest house, we walk around back to see a frozen pond nestled in a little valley. It's surrounded by long, deep, tree-dappled backyards on three sides, but the winter-bare branches of a wooded area line the far shore. People are ice-skating, and a handful of others stand around a crackling blaze in a firepit nearby.

"That fire looks nice and cozy after being outside so long," Lexi says, then turns to meet my gaze. "Let's go down and warm up."

We could warm up easier and faster by just getting in the truck and heading back to our heated buildings on Main Street, but I don't point that out. I'm not sure why. Instead, I lower my toolbox to the snow where I can pick it back up later and follow her down a snow-covered hillside to the gathering below.

As we approach the small crowd by the fire, she seems acquainted with everyone there, and introduces me. A couple of men say they know my father and were sorry to hear about his diagnosis. I give a small 'thanks', and am glad when the subject changes—someone asks what brings us to the neighborhood.

Lexi looks a little sheepish—except for the lady who requested visitors, we've been keeping our wish-granting pretty low-profile, so she seems caught off guard. Finally she answers, "We were just doing a little project at Kathryn and Hank's house. But don't tell them it was us—it's a Christmas surprise."

A gray-haired woman across the firepit grins. "Don't tell me you put in a ramp for her." She claps gloved hands together. "Oh my goodness, that's just the best Christmas gift. You're a couple of angels."

Two things I take in:

I make a good living in Chicago and so do most of the people I know—so if anyone in my circle needed a wheelchair ramp, it wouldn't be a big imposition to get one. I guess I've forgotten that many people here struggle in that way, and that a little generosity can mean a lot. Hell, maybe it *is* a sort of magic. I just never thought about it that way before.

And people truly *like* my dad. Everyone who knows him seems to feel genuine affection for him. So whatever happened after I left, he became...better. A better man. And maybe I'm suddenly a little sorry I missed out on that.

"Wanna go skatin'?" asks a middle-aged guy in an old-fashioned plaid hunting cap, the kind with flaps over the ears. He points to a tiny shed near the pond, where a bench sits near the open door, the ground around it strewn with people's boots and shoes. "Got plenty o' skates in there in perty much ever' size."

Lexi tilts her head, clearly as surprised by this as I am. "Will, where on earth did you get a bunch of ice skates?"

"My grandson used to play hockey at a rink up in Crescent Springs, and when I heard they was replacin' their rental skates, I asked what they'd take fer the old ones – just thought it'd be fun fer folks to come skate here on the pond. And they gave 'em to me fer free!"

Lexi looks up at me. "What do you think? Wanna skate?"

"Haven't done it in a long time," I inform her.

"I haven't done it *ever*," she confesses. "But I'm willing to try if you are."

We find skates in the shed and as we sit changing into them on the bench, she asks, "So did you skate out at your farm as a kid? Or somewhere else?"

"Yep, at the farm," I say. "On a pond behind the house—real shallow, so it froze easy. I got skates for Christmas when I was around nine."

"How did you learn?"

I laugh at the memory. "Dad would pull me around on the skates, holding both my hands. But he *wasn't* on skates – just had his workboots on. So it was the blind leading the blind, but I caught on eventually. Only did it for a couple of winters until I outgrew the skates." We never replaced them because by then things were bad, both financially and otherwise. "But it was fun while it lasted."

"You're gonna have to help me," she says as we both stand up on the thin blades, wobbly. She reaches out to grab my gloved hand in her mittened one to keep from falling and I squeeze her fingers in mine.

Then I toss her a grin. "Help with wishes. Help with skating. You're lucky I came back to town when I did."

It feels good when she smiles back at me to say, "Guess I am."

Still holding hands, we ease our way onto the ice like a couple of newborn calves learning to walk for the first time. Her ankles bend and I put an arm around her waist to hold her up as I tug her along with me.

"You're terrible at this," I say, laughing.

"You're right about that, too," she tells me, letting out a pretty giggle of her own.

As I guide her around on the ice, it's impossible not to feel her nearness and that I like it. I like *her*. And if things were different, if I were staying here, maybe I would ask her out. I've been reluctant to let myself even consider that, yet as we've spent more time together, she's made this strange visit home a lot more interesting, and a lot more fun, than I could have imagined.

But this isn't my real life. It's just...an odd vacation. It's my past colliding with my present. It's filling my time while I'm stuck in my old hometown in better ways than I expected—even when she's making me wear a Santa hat.

Only...is she starting to actually care about me?

And is she the same soft-hearted girl I once stood up at a dance?

I guess there's a reason for my reluctance—I wouldn't want anyone getting hurt when the time comes for me to leave.

So this can't really be any more than it is right now: a nice friendship, sometimes sprinkled with a little flirtation.

Besides, my father is dying. My father is dying right when I'm starting to realize that I no longer hate him. And maybe I never really did because hate is just the flip side of love, right? I'm juggling a lot, more than I even expected when Wally summoned me home.

And so right now, I'm going to just enjoy this moment, enjoy the fact that I'm ice-skating on a sunny day with a cute girl whose attitude about life I admire, enjoy the way it feels to hold her against me. A little time away from the drama is good—and it's okay if I don't think too hard about anything but the skating and the warmth and the laughter.

"We're gonna have to get up a little speed," I inform her then, "if this is gonna turn into actual skating. That's the only way to get your balance. Kind of the same way you learn to ride a bike."

"Okay." She sounds nervous but brave, still wobbling along next to me.

"I'm gonna let go of you and just pull you along by your hands, all right?"

She nods. "I'll try."

I release my grip—even though the closeness was nice—and situate myself in front of her, holding both her hands in mine. I skate backward, slowly, having found it is, indeed, like riding a bike—and I take her with me. She's stiff-legged, but still on her feet.

"There ya go," I say. "You're doing it."

"I am?" she asks, wide-eyed and pretty, brown locks falling around her face from beneath her thick, knitted hat.

I nod. "Whenever you're ready, try lifting one skate, just a little, to see if you can start shifting your weight back and forth."

"Don't let go of me," she pleads.

"No worries. I've got you."

She raises one skate slightly, then puts it back on the ice before lifting the other.

"Hey, hey," I say in celebration. "There ya go."

I'm still the one propelling us even though I'm skating backward, and I increase our speed just slightly as she finds a rhythm.

"You're doing great," I assure her.

She's smiling at me, clearly enjoying her success, and I'm smiling back, noticing little flecks of gold in her blue eyes that I've never spotted before and how her cheeks are pinker than usual from the cold. She looks gorgeous.

That's when my skate hits a divot in the ice I couldn't

see coming and I lose my balance to go tumbling backward, unwittingly pulling her down on top of me. We land in a tangled embrace, her body pressed to mine from chest to thigh. It's like our Christmas tree debacle last night, but better—no pointy branches—and even through our winter coats, I feel the shape of her, the warmth of her, as my arms close loosely around her. Our faces, our mouths, are only a few inches apart.

I want to kiss her. It would be the easiest thing in the world to do.

But instead I say, "Not sure we're quite ready for the Olympic team yet."

The sound of her sweet laugh runs all through me as I ask, "Getting cold?"

"Mmm hmm."

"Ready to give this up yet or do you want to keep trying?"

As she considers the question, I realize maybe it's more weighted than I intended, that a person could take a double-meaning from it if they chose.

"Both?" she answers. "It's fun doing this with you, but... I'm not very good at it."

"You're fine at it," I tell her, not quite sure what we're talking about anymore. Ice-skating or walking that fine line between casual attraction and something stronger. "But maybe we should get our boots back on and go warm up, huh?"

After a moment of suspecting I see the same questions dancing in those blue eyes, she nibbles her lower lip and answers, "That would probably be wise."

December 17

Lexi

I spend all day working in the shop, but part of me remains back on that pond yesterday, balancing on the thin blades of ice skates that felt like walking a tightrope of sorts. All around me, the shop is buzzing, people are putting wishes in the box and ringing out their purchases with Dara, and all my favorite Christmas tunes fill the air—but I'm stuck in that moment when learning to skate felt more like learning to navigate a tricky relationship.

It's only when the afternoon rush dies down and Dara and I are left alone, her behind the counter and me wiping down the coffee bar, that she asks, "What's with you today? You seem like you're somewhere else. Are you still caught up in granting Christmas wishes or...is it something more?"

"He almost kissed me."

Her jaw drops. "What?"

"We were ice-skating and we fell down together and he almost kissed me. But then he stopped. And I somehow felt...childish. Like...for him a kiss would just be a kiss, but he knew that for me it would be more, and so he didn't. And it's probably for the best anyway." I end by trying to head-shake it away as nothing, almost sorry I said anything.

Her eyes widen with doubt, though. "Is it? For the best?"

I nod. "He's going back to Chicago sooner or later—probably sooner."

"Don't be stupid," she tells me then.

I lower my chin, giving her a look. "It's stupid to protect my heart?"

"No, it's stupid to squander an opportunity to be with someone you're connecting with, all over the fear of how it might end. I mean, who knows what the future holds? None of us."

"Well, you're forgetting something here. He's the one who didn't kiss me. He's the one who decided to squander an opportunity. And maybe I'm wrong about why. But whatever his reason, he didn't do it. Maybe...he's just not attracted to me in that way."

"He sent you pie."

"Huh?" I squint.

"He sent you pie. I still say it's like sending a woman a drink at a bar. It's a silent invitation for more. It's announcing, 'Hey, I'm into you.'"

"Or maybe it was just pie."

"Want my advice?" she asks.

I flash widened eyes her way. "Even if I don't, I'm pretty sure you're gonna give it to me."

"I think you just play this out. I mean, you obviously like his company and he obviously likes yours or he wouldn't be out doing all this wish fulfillment with you. So enjoy having him around and see where it goes. And maybe...well, maybe the next time you fall into his arms, *you* kiss *him*."

At this, I make a face. "I'm not really the kiss-instigating type. I've always been shy about that—I prefer the guy to make the first move."

"Well, maybe he's got a lot on his mind. Maybe if a pretty girl kissed him, he'd realize she's incredible and it would change *everything*."

"And if it *didn't* make him realize that?"

She shrugs. "You get a hopefully toe-curling kiss out of it. A delicious memory. And then life goes on. Nothing ventured, nothing gained."

"Easy for you to say," I tell her. For all her bold suggestions, I'm not sure she would handle the situation any differently than me. And now it's time to change the subject. "Moving on, is everything in place for tonight?"

She nods, changing gears along with me. "Everyone is meeting here at five, we're closing early, and I printed off copies of the song lyrics."

I smile. "Awesome." The last wish on my to-do list is caroling at Eve Lindley's house, a few blocks away up Main, followed by a right on Corinth Avenue. Dara and I will be joined by Helen and almost a dozen members of her church choir, who she pressed into service when I asked.

She also arranged to go in late to her evening shift at the manor so she could join us. We plan to sing our way there and beyond, including a stop at Dara's house so Judy can have visitors, as well. "This is gonna be great."

"Did you invite Travis?" Dara asks.

I shake my head. "He's more than done his part when it comes to wish-granting. And I'm almost sure he'd say no to this."

"He's said no to other things, too, but then given in when you pushed him a little."

Even so, I only shrug, still lost in the disappointment of the kiss that wasn't.

The shortest day of the year is but a few calendar-page flips away, so darkness comes early as the bundled-up carolers amass at the Christmas Box. I offer hot chocolate fortification, both for now and to take when we go.

Across the street, Travis is busy at work on cabinets. I know the wishes have pulled him away from that, and he's still visiting his father every day, too. I'm also aware he didn't come over for coffee this morning.

It's only been a day, but I already feel a subtle distance between us that I hate. I'm afraid I've gotten attached to him. I'm afraid I might be hurt when he leaves, with or without any kissing.

But...could Dara be right? Should I just keep enjoying the moments with him—unconcerned about what happens next?

And what if my original wish for him needs more help, like the ones we found in the box? After all, he's not *officially* rescinded his anti-Christmas stance yet. I know he's felt Christmas in his heart in more ways than one lately, but that doesn't mean the star wish has come completely true. Glancing across at him through the plate-glass windows, I resolve to forget about romance, forget about love, and remember that from the moment he came back into my life, what I most wanted was to change his mind about Christmas—and that work isn't quite done yet.

"Is everyone here?" Helen calls to the group milling about the store. "Are we ready to commence caroling?"

I make a split-second decision. "Hang on a minute. Dara, can you hand out the song sheets? We'll go as soon as I get back from a speedy errand." With that, I snatch up my coat, and before I can stop myself, I'm out the door and crossing the street in the wintry dusk.

As I come bursting into the Lucas Building, Travis and Marley both look up.

"Wish-granting duty calls," I announce. "Grab your coat and gloves."

Understandably, he looks confused, woodworking plane paused in hand. "What wish?"

"Caroling at Eve Lindley's house. There's a group across the street waiting to go."

He shoots me a look. "C'mon, Lex. I already built a wheelchair ramp. I even snuck a Christmas tree up the road in the dark. And I decorated cookies because you're bad at it. But it sounds like you've got this one covered without me. I'm no singer."

"Neither am I," I tell him. "But it's a nice thing to do and you got me into this wish-fulfilling business, so you're going with me. You don't even have to sing if you don't want to."

"What about the dog?" he argues, falling back on what has become his usual excuse. "I feel like I've been neglecting her."

We both look to a perfectly mellow-looking Marley. "She'll survive for an hour." And with that I pluck up his coat, currently draped over the counter in back, and hold it out to him.

"This'll only take an hour?" he asks, eyes narrowed on me skeptically.

"Yes." Give or take. Actually, I have no idea, but what I'm pretty certain of is that once he's there, he'll enjoy it—because that seems to be how it goes with him.

A few minutes later, I notice he forgot his winter hat, so I've plopped that same Santa hat back on his head, and we're moving up Main Street carrying lit candles with tinfoil holders, singing *Deck the Halls*. People are peeking through curtains and stepping out on porches, smiling as we pass. The Christmas joy is spreading from us and among us, and when I glance up at Travis beside me during a fa-la-la, I find him singing, too.

When the song ends, before we break into *What Child is This?*, I whisper up to him, "Are you as miserable as you thought you'd be?"

"It's not awful," he whispers back.

The words warm me up inside despite the cold—and I don't even mind when it begins to snow.

Travis

After caroling, I ask Lexi to grab a bite with me at Winterburger.

As we sit eating, we talk about all we've accomplished the past few days. "I know we still have a few loose ends to tie up," she says, "but it's been pretty great making so many people happy."

I can't argue the point, and it reminds me... "Hey, have you heard anything about the ramp? Did they like it?"

Her eyes brighten across the table from me. "Yes! I got a text from Carol Ann this morning. She suspected I might have something to do with it, but I didn't confirm or deny. She said her mom and dad are so grateful to their secret Santa. Kathyrn's looking forward to spring so she can spend time birdwatching in her yard again. And it's going to be so much easier for Hank to get her over to Carol Ann's for Christmas dinner."

The truth is, hearing that something I did is making such an impact on someone's life kind of fills me up inside. But I keep it simple with, "That's great news," as I dip a fry in ketchup. Then I look past Lexi, my gaze drawn to the big windows. "Wow, snow's really coming down out there."

"Ugh," she says.

I stop eating long enough to pull out my phone and check the forecast—then I blow out a sigh. "Looks like it's gonna be another snowy evening. Half a foot by midnight."

Lexi's eyes widen yet again, but not in a happy way this time. "What's going on here? We never get this much snow in December. If I weren't such a glass-half-full kind of person, I might believe the universe didn't want my shop to succeed."

She once confided in me that she was worried about the future of the Christmas Box, but she hasn't brought it up again other than to complain when it snows. "So how *is* business?"

"Fine," she answers, sounding conflicted, "but it needs to be better. If we were as busy on the snow days as on the non-snow days, I think we'd be okay. But all this snow has thrown a cold, white, frosty wrench into my plans."

I already know it takes a lot to bring Lexi Hargrove down, so the despair I hear in her voice makes me ask, "Are the prospects really that bad? How dire is the situation?"

Pressing her lips together as she weighs the question, she finally replies, "Only time will tell, but...I think it's pretty dire. And if I lose the place this fast..." She stops, shakes her head. "It's more than a business to me, Trav—it's a legacy. My family has had a business on Main Street for a hundred years until the last ten. I wanted this for me, but also for them." The expression on her face is grim. "We've been open less than a month, but at this point I'm not sure we'll make it through a second one."

Okay, that's worse than I expected. I suffer the intense urge to give her a long, warm hug—but the table between us keeps me from it.

Which is good, since taking things further between us still seems like a bad idea.

But I feel terrible for her. "That's tough, Lex. But... maybe it's not too late for things to turn around?" It's all I can think of to say.

Her long sigh relays her discouragement, though. "It's a week until Christmas. And it's snowing like crazy, which means opening tomorrow will barely be worth the electricity to keep the lights on. But...who knows, right? Maybe some miracle will occur when I least expect it."

Despite how dejected she appears, that light of hers is still trying to shine—she's attempting to keep the faith even though logic is challenging her.

And that's when her phone trills the notes to "We Wish You a Merry Christmas"—apparently her ringtone. She glances down at it on the table and says, "It's Helen. Do you mind?"

I shake my head, encouraging her to answer.

A few seconds later, I hear Helen's booming voice ask, "Are you still with Travis?"

"Yeah," Lexi tells her.

"Oh, good. I need your help, both of you."

"What's wrong?"

"It's this blasted snowstorm," her voice echoes. "I don't know if you've looked outside in the last few minutes, but it's pretty much blizzard conditions out there, right when we were finally set to get our tree up here at the manor and have our tree-trimming party. Glen was ready to head to the tree lot in Holly Ridge, but old tires are making his truck worthless in the snow. I wonder if you and Travis would be willing to take his pickup and get the tree. The residents have been waiting for this and it keeps getting postponed time after time. They have so little to look forward to—I hate to keep disappointing them."

"Of course we will," I answer loud enough for Helen to hear.

"But Helen," Lexi says while peering across the table at me. "Won't the tree lot be closed?"

"One step ahead of you," I hear Helen reply. "Chuck, the tree guy, lives right next door to the lot. Just honk when you get there. He's already picked us out a nine-foot Scotch pine and has it waiting. It's already paid for and everything."

"Tell her we're on our way," I say.

I had set my dumb Santa hat beside me in the booth as soon as we stepped into the burger place, but now I accept my fate, pick it up, and plop it back on my head. "A Santa's work is never done around here."

The roads to Holly Ridge are terrible, but my tough old Ford gets us there. Helen was right—it's turned into a blizzard—so I insist Lexi stay inside as Chuck and I maneuver the big tree into the truck bed.

When we turn into the lot at the manor a little while later, Helen and Brent are both waiting inside the sliding glass doors in their coats, Helen clapping her hands at the sight of us. I pull right up to the entrance.

"The cavalry has arrived," Helen declares, stepping out with Brent to greet us in the swirling snow.

"You head back inside," I tell her, "and take Lexi with you. Brent, can you help me get this monster inside?"

"You got it," he says, and few minutes later, we're

toting a snow-covered tree down the hall, weaving a path between the familiar faces wandering about on four wheels.

"Hey there, Shannon," I call, spotting her in the doorway to her room.

"You brought our tree," she says. And I can actually understand her! At last!

"Yep," I say, smiling over at her.

"Oooh, the tree is here." I look over to see Gabbi through an open door, bright-eyed at the sight as she tends to one of the residents.

Helen and Lexi wait near the nurse's station, Helen directing us. "Right around the corner and into the cafeteria," she tells me, pointing. "We've got the stand set up and waiting."

We struggle a little to get the tall evergreen in place, and some of the residents gather around, watching, all while Bing Crosby croons "It's Beginning to Look a Lot Like Christmas" over the room's speakers. Once it's up, Helen oohs and ahhs. "What a nice tree. I'll have to give Chuck a big thank you."

When I meet her gaze, I can see just how deep her happiness runs. "Thanks to you, young Mr. Hutchins, all these fine folks can finally have the party they've been looking forward to. You're saving the day and we can't express our gratitude enough."

Damn, I think I'm actually blushing—mainly because everyone is staring at me, acting like I'm some kind of hero. "It's nothing, Helen. Really."

But she's not having it. "Oh, it's something all right. It's a very big something. And now we can thank you by including you and Lexi in our party."

Oh crap. "That's not necessary," I'm quick to assure her.

"But we want to," she insists.

I insist back. "This is for the residents—we don't need to intrude."

"Your dad is having a good day," she says, trying to entice me. "Wide awake. When I told him you were coming to the party, his eyes lit up."

Well, that got me in the gut. Guess I'm staying. "Just don't ask me to carve the roast beast," I say, and she and Lexi crack up laughing.

"All right, we've got a lot to do, people," Helen says, flying into work mode. "We need to start getting the residents in here, and let the food service folks know it's time to bring the refreshments. Travis, maybe you and Lexi can start stringing the lights on the tree—they're in that box over there." She points.

I head to the box and fish out a strand, plugging it into a socket. When the lights come on, I climb a step stool already out for the occasion. "Though I don't like admitting this," I confess to Lexi as she helps untangle lights, "I guess I *do* have a lot in common with The Grinch Who Stole Christmas. I mean, I never stole it exactly, but I wanted nothing to do with it. And now I'm suddenly the guy who delivers the tree in a Santa hat."

"Twice," she says.

"Huh?" I pause in place to ask.

"You delivered a tree to Mikayla the other night, too."

I give a little shiver, half teasing, half real. "What's happened to me?"

Below me, she's draping her end of the strand on some lower branches. "You've embraced the Christmas spirit," she says like it's nothing, eyes on her task.

"That's not true," I argue instinctively. Because it just sounds so...corny to me. "All I've done is get some people the things they needed to have a good holiday and lent a helping hand."

"All while wearing a Santa hat. And that, my friend, is the Christmas spirit."

Lexi

Burl Ives is telling us to have a holly, jolly Christmas over the speakers as Helen and I help some of the residents hang non-breakable ornaments on the tree. Travis sits talking to his dad at a nearby table, both of them sporting Santa hats. I take a break and walk over, point my camera phone at them, and tell them to smile. I'll text it to Travis later and he'll be glad he has it one day. Tom looks even thinner than he did at the festival—or maybe it's because he's only in pajamas now, with a blanket folded over his lap.

Soon enough, Helen has asked everyone to get a cup of punch, and then makes a toast. "To our friends, Travis and Lexi, who brought us this beautiful tree through the storm and have stayed to help us celebrate the season. And now," she says, narrowing her gaze on the unwitting Santa standing next to me, "I'd like to ask Travis to honor us by placing our star on top."

He's giving her a what-do-you-think-you're-doing? look. "Helen," he says, his low voice a warning. "I told you, no carving the roast beast."

"It's not roast beast," she says, pretending not to understand. "It's a star. Now come on."

Reluctantly, he steps up and takes a shiny gold star from her hands. That's the thing I've noticed about Travis —though it's often done with a characteristic reluctance, perhaps from years of trauma, he always steps up.

And as he climbs on to the stool and reaches over to place the star carefully atop the tree, I feel like we've come full circle—a few short weeks ago, I placed a star on a tree with a wish, and now I see more evidence of that wish coming true by the very placing of *this* star.

A few minutes later as the party rollicks on, he arrives at my side with a slice of pumpkin pie on a plate. "Pie, Mrs. Claus?"

I take it, remembering that other piece of pie from him. "Thank you, Mr. Claus."

He draws back to look at me and I realize I've just accidentally suggested we're an old married couple. But, thankfully, that's not what he tuned into. You got it wrong. I'm Mr. Scrooge, Mr. Grinch. I'm a mean one. Remember?"

But I just shake my head. "Not anymore. You're totally Mr. Claus now—don't even try to deny it."

And he doesn't get a chance to before Mariah Carey's *All I Want For Christmas Is You* suddenly blasts through the speakers and Helen calls out, "Let's all dance!"

Of course, most people are in wheelchairs, but that doesn't stop her—she takes the hands of an elderly lady and begins to swing her arms in a dancing motion. Gabbi follows suit by grabbing another chair's handles and turning it this way and that to the music.

Travis's dad sits near me nibbling on a cookie, so I turn to him. "May I have this dance, Mr. Hutchins?"

"Now, I'd be a fool to turn down an invitation from such a pretty girl," he says, so I set my pie on a table and take his hands in mine, moving us both to the happy beat.

Nearby I see Travis, indeed no longer a mean one when it comes to Christmas, bend down over an old lady holding a babydoll. He whispers something in her ear that makes her smile. Then he takes hold of her wheelchair handles and dances her around the Christmas tree.

Christmas. Magic.

It's late by the time we leave. The snow is deep on untouched streets, but it's stopped falling. Dressed in a mantel of white that glistens beneath streetlights, Winterberry has become a still, quiet Thomas Kincaid painting.

We make the only tire tracks in the snow as we head back toward town. "Looks like everybody else stayed home tonight, warm and safe from the bad weather," Travis says.

"Can't blame them, but...I can't think of anyplace I'd have rather been," I reply. "I'm glad we braved the storm. It was a nice night." I smile over at him and he smiles back.

"Yeah, I'm glad we did it, too."

As we roll onto Main Street and Travis pulls the old truck to his usual spot along the curb, I look out on my little town in wonder. "In all my life," I tell him, "I've never seen Main Street like this."

"Like what?" he asks, but the softness of his voice tells me he already knows because he sees it, too.

Not one car has sullied the fresh-fallen snow on Main. To see the old buildings rising up from both sides of the pristinely snow-covered thoroughfare, the Christmas lights glowing in windows, is unexpectedly beautiful.

"Perfect after a snowfall," I answer anyway. "Like a meadow or a hillside, but it's Main Street. There's always *someone* on the road, *someone* leaving tire tracks. And then the snowplows come, and it gets slushy and dirty. But this... this is as perfect and unblemished as a little old town could ever look, don't you think?"

"Let's get out," he suggests. "Soak it in."

I plant my snowboots in ankle-deep snow, almost sorry to make footprints, but there's no avoiding it. Our truck doors slam, and a moment later, we stand side by side, taking in the splendor.

The air is cold but clear after the storm, leaving the sense that the wind swept away anything bad to leave Winterberry crisp and clean. Colored lights on the tree in the park glisten even through the snow adorning its limbs, and the greenery wrapped around streetlamps is snow-covered, too, but held strong through the blizzard.

"It's a Christmas card," I say. Then I pull out my phone and snap a picture. Which I already know I'm going to frame on the wall of my shop—well, if my shop exists beyond another month or two. But I refuse to think about that now.

Back in Winterburger with Travis, when Helen called, I realized I just have to let it go. I have to take my own advice once and for all and simply believe. I have to embrace each day, each moment, for what it brings. That approach to life has always served me well—I just occasionally have to remind myself of that.

So I embrace it—all of it. I embrace the uncertainty. And I embrace the winter beauty, and the sparkling snow, and the silence that never seems so pronounced as after a snowfall when nothing stirs. Main Street belongs only to the two of us right now—it's a private place no one will ever see the way we're seeing it in this moment.

"We should do something," Travis breaks that silence to suggest, "that you've never done on Main Street before and will never get to do again."

I look over at him, intrigued by the notion. "Like?"

The expression on his face becomes a playful one. "Wanna make snow angels?"

We exchange giddy grins, then without further words, we both lie down in the snow in the middle of Main Street, our heads together, out bodies pointing in opposite directions. It feels almost surreal as the cold seeps through my blue jeans while I move my arms and legs back and forth, peering up through the steam of my own breath at a clear, dark sky. "Look," I say. "Up."

"Wow," he replies, his voice warm near my ear. The storm's departure has allowed a million stars to come out. "Nature's Christmas lights," he says.

And that's it. I'm in love with him. There's no getting around it.

And no worrying over it, either. I'm fully in the moment and this moment is one of the best of my life.

We lay silently peering upward for a few long, blissful minutes until he says, on a small laugh, "I'm pretty cold. We should probably get up."

I'm cold, too, but just wanted this to last. "Carefully, though," I tell him. "So our angels will be intact."

We get to our feet, side by side, and now, instead of looking up, we look down.

"They're perfect," I say.

"*This night* was perfect," Travis replies.

"This moment's perfect," I tell him.

"*You're* perfect."

Okay, I was cold, but that warms me up fast. I turn to gaze up at the handsome man beside me, my heart racing. I think of Dara's advice. That if I have the chance to kiss him, I should just do it, without a care for what tomorrow brings.

Of course, initiating a kiss comes with the horrible risk of rejection. But...I want to kiss him so badly. The desire oozes slow and hot through my veins. And what if this opportunity never comes again? *Embrace the uncertainty.*

And as I begin to lift on my tiptoes, starting to make that daring move...he does it first. He lifts one gloved hand to my cheek and lowers a soft, sweet kiss to my lips.

Silence. Warmth. Heaven. All on Main Street at midnight.

"You should do that again," I whisper.

He does. But this time the kiss grows deeper, his mouth moving over mine in a way that spreads through me like embers igniting into a flame. We stand making out in the middle of Main Street until I'm lost in it, thinking of nothing but the heat of his body against mine—and forgetting that I was ever cold.

Once upon a time, as I waited for my escort to the Christmas Ball, I fantasized that maybe, just maybe, he would kiss me goodnight. That never happened, but as I melt into Travis Hutchins' strong arms, all I know is that it was worth the wait.

And then, when we break from the kissing, his breath comes warm in my ear. "This is nice. But we should probably say goodnight."

A *whoosh* of disappointment rushes the length of my body. We should?

Yet then I get it. This is like at the pond, more of that stuff I'm not very good at. He's feeling me out. Seeing if I protest, if I'm okay with a casual connection that won't last beyond his visit home.

Dara would say I should just go for it. That would be the epitome of living in the moment and embracing the uncertainty, wouldn't it?

But I have to remember my heart here, and try to protect it at least a little. Don't I?

So even though it's almost physically painful, I answer the same way I did at the pond, my voice leaving me quieter than intended. "That would probably be wise."

With that, he takes my mitten-covered hand and walks me to my door through the snow. He again lifts his palm to my cheek, and this time he kisses the other. Then he turns to go.

I don't want the moment to be over. But that's the

problem with moments, and it's why you have to be in them: they don't last. They drift away, one into another into another, and you can only hold on to them with memory.

I stand outside the door to my shop and watch him walk back across the street to disappear inside the Lucas Building. And the moment is gone.

But I feel that kiss on my cheek for a very long time.

December 19

Travis

I wait in Winterburger for my to-go order, a few of the booths and tables around me filled with lunch customers.

As I plodded up the snowy sidewalk to get here, the town felt entirely different than it had just hours before. Snowplows have come through, scraping away snow angels and leaving behind slush, and boot prints have pressed down any snow on the sidewalk not yet cleared away by shopkeepers. Kissing Lexi in the middle of the street last night feels almost like a dream.

But I know it really happened. Even though I tried to resist the urge.

I wanted to ask her to invite me in. I almost did. But same as when we were ice-skating, I'm not sure I should start something with her I can't finish.

Though on the other hand, much as I hate to admit it, something about this place has started feeling almost like home again—and not in the bad way it once did, but in a warmer sense maybe I can only appreciate now, as an adult. Or maybe that feeling is about the woman who runs the Christmas Box. Maybe she's just gotten inside me and made me begin to wonder what in Chicago I'm in such a hurry to get back to.

I've always been happy there, and I make a comfortable living. I have friends, and interests. I belong to a classic car club. I play pickup basketball every Tuesday. But...when was the last time I dated a girl who gets under my skin the way Lexi does, makes me laugh like Lexi does, warms up everything inside me like Lexi does, makes me see the world through through a more hopeful, giving lens the way Lexi does?

Yep, I should have asked her to invite me in.

That's when Nick exits the kitchen into the dining room to take a seat, still in his apron, a soda cup in hand. Must be on a break.

The sight of him reminds me of the one wish on our list I haven't done anything about yet. Christmas is coming fast, and I don't have a plan, but I decide to wing it.

Uninvited, I slide into the booth seat across from him. Then I lean closer and speak in a low tone, like I'm some kind of holiday secret agent. "Listen, don't ask me how I know this, but if your son is thinking of proposing, Christmas would be a great time. And if he's not, maybe he should. But you didn't hear this from me."

I wait for the guy to tell me to mind my own business, or maybe look at me like I'm a lunatic—since that would be fair. But instead, concern knits his brow. "Is Marissa getting tired of waiting? I mean, I don't blame her. Cash loves her—he's just..."

When he trails off, I plow ahead, not needing to know any more about his family's personal affairs than I already somehow do. "Look, I have no idea," I tell him. "And I've said all I can say. We never had this conversation."

"What conversation?" he replies smoothly, like a fellow spy.

"Order up for Travis," Gail announces behind the counter.

I get up, grab my burger bag, then head toward the door. But then I stop and look back at Nick. "Hey," I tell him, "if I don't see you in the next few days, have a merry Christmas."

"You, too," he says.

And I walk out into the cold shaking my head. Since when do I wish people a merry Christmas? Who am I?

I shrug off the questions as I head down the street to my truck, though—because I have other, more important things on my mind. The woman at the Christmas shop, for instance. The fact that maybe it really is failing, and the look in her eyes when she told me that. And I'm also dreading the end with Dad. It's all suddenly a little overwhelming.

Though back in high school, Mr. West once counseled me that when you're going through something hard, you should just take one day at a time. "Concentrate on the steps in front of you today, not the whole journey," he said. It stuck with me and helped me get through the rest of senior year, and then leaving home. Maybe I need to heed that advice now.

I walk into the manor toting my Winterburger bag and start my usual bob and weave through the residents roaming the hallways.

"Hi, Dottie," I say, spotting her as I move past. Only then do I notice the anguish in her gaze and realize she's not carrying her babydoll.

Just like the last time this happened, a protective fury rises in me, making it so I can barely see straight. And also just like last time, I spy a familiar old robe down the corridor—the man wearing it padding away in worn slippers, her "baby" dangling from his fingertips.

What is it with this guy? What's it gonna take for him to leave Dottie alone?

I make a beeline toward him, determined to make him listen this time.

Though it's only as I step into his path, only as he looks at me with that strange, innocent little smile, that I remember what Helen told me: He doesn't know what he's doing; he means no harm. And I realize that no amount of yelling at this guy is gonna make any difference.

Probably no amount of kindness or reasoning will, either, sadly—but it at least stops me from flying into a rage in the middle of Bluegrass Manor.

"Hey, Henry," I say, having long since learned his name. "You can't keep taking Dottie's doll." I reach down, gently removing it from his grasp. And for Dottie's sake, because she's watching all this, I make sure to hold the doll upright between both hands. "It's very important to her. She loves it very much. It's hers, not yours—okay?"

In the weeks I've been coming here, I've yet to hear Henry utter a single word and today is no different. He just keeps giving me that same empty smile.

Walking back to Dottie with the doll, I know I haven't fixed anything long term, but...all I can do is deal with the steps in front of me today "Here you go," I tell her, gently lowering the doll into her arms. Cradling it, she strokes its little face with withered fingers.

"See, she's okay," I tell the old woman soothingly. "She's all right." And as I stand over her, I feel the strange absurdity of the moment: How did I get here?

Maybe everyone here wonders that sometimes.

That's when Helen comes rushing up from behind. "Ah, Travis to the rescue once again," she says, sounding relieved. "I was just on my way to deal with that situation, but I appreciate you beating me to it."

After she does a sort of silent check-in with Dottie, rubbing her arm and giving her a comforting smile, she and I start walking together.

"Is there no way to stop that guy from taking the baby?"

I realize too late that I've called it a baby, like Dottie's reality has overtaken mine, but Helen seems entirely unfazed.

She just shakes her head. "Can't lock them in their rooms—they have to have what little freedom we can give them here." Then she lets out a sigh. "I don't know why he's started doing that lately, but we're keeping an eye on the situation as best we can. We don't like the stress it puts Dottie under any better than you do."

She sounds so calm the whole time she speaks—she *always* sounds calm. I turn to peer down at her as we make a jagged path between wheelchairs. "How do you do it, Helen?"

I can tell by her gentle smile and knowing eyes that she understands exactly what I'm talking about, even as she feigns ignorance."Do what?"

"You *know* what."

At this, she only shrugs, coming clean. "Someone has to," she tells me. "It's my calling in life, I suppose. So many people become...forgotten here. It's heartbreaking, really. As I've told you, I'm often the one with them when they take their last breaths. It shouldn't be that way—everyone should feel loved. But for those who aren't, I'm happy to fill that role."

It hits me that my dad could have been one of those people and I'm glad he's not; I'm glad he knows I'm here for him. Even if I'm dreading when that time comes.

"Isn't it hard on you?" I ask. "Dealing with so much death?"

"I've grown used to it over time. I see it like someone going on a trip, or moving away. They're here with me for a while, and then they go, with me wishing them good travels, and perhaps missing them when they're gone, but knowing they're just someplace else now." With that, she reaches down and takes my hand in hers, giving it a warm squeeze as she smiles up at me. "Your dad's having another good day today. Still not eating a lot, but maybe that scrumptious-smelling burger will change his mind. Go have a nice visit with him."

As we part ways, I sense that her smile for that last part was a bit forced. Maybe she'll miss my father. Maybe she's warning me the end is near. I can't decipher it and resolve not to try too hard. One day, one step, at a time.

Half an hour later I've watched Dad take only a few bites of his burger and pick at the fries while I've been telling him about the wishes Lexi and I helped grant the last few days.

"That's real nice, son," he says softly. "I'm proud of you for being so good to others."

But I'm uncomfortable taking credit and point out, "It's really *her* making it all happen."

His look of doubt catches me off guard. "Don't sound that way to me. You made the box. It was your idea to read the wishes. You made the wheelchair ramp and toted the tree."

And all that's true, but still I insist, "I wouldn't have done any of it without her, though. She kind of brings out the best in me. Even as her business is failing, she's spending all her time looking out for other people."

"She's a nice young lady. Sorry to hear about her shop."

"I want to do more to help," I tell him, "but this is one thing I don't know how to fix."

"Need to get more folks in there," Dad says, stating the obvious.

"Got any ideas on how?" I don't expect him to come up with anything—for a guy with advanced brain cancer, I'm amazed enough that he's sitting up talking to me entirely lucidly—but the words left me out of frustration.

"Shame ya can't just point a big arrow to her place from I 75," he muses. Winterberry sits directly off the major expressway that runs from Michigan to Florida. "I remember a time when billboards lined the interstate, but these days I think there's a bunch of rules and regulations around it." He shrugs. "Reckon it does look nicer without, though."

Dad's rambling now, but it gives me an idea. Probably a far-fetched one that would never work, something that would take way longer to pull together than I have.

But I hear myself asking him anyway, "Does Richard Hargis still own the farm where we used to visit him when I was a kid?" He was my father's boss, running the construction company where Dad worked until it went under, starting our financial troubles.

"I believe he does," Dad answers. I remember fishing there, in a pond so close to 75 that it felt like the cars were whizzing past right next to me. It wasn't a peaceful spot, despite the woods and pastures in all other directions—but it suddenly seems like the exact place I need.

Although now that I'm thinking through it, there would be other big things to figure out—I need more than just the place. And even so, I hear myself trying to dredge up ways it could work, no matter how crazy the idea probably is.

"Am I remembering correctly that his kids were both artistic?"

Dad squints slightly, cocking me a sideways glance. "Um, yeah, think so. Both a few years ahead of you in school if I recall."

I nod. "Do they still live locally?"

With that same questioning look, he replies, "Believe his daughter built a house on the property, near his."

Well, this feels like a long shot, but for Lexi, it's better than no shot at all. "Still got his number?"

"Reckon it's in the phone book at the house, on the shelf above the microwave." Then he grins. "And maybe I just got a notion about what's percolating in your brain. If I'm right, and if Richard gives you any guff, you tell him it's my dying wish." He finishes on a wink and I'm still astounded he can be as stoic—and even jovial—about his impending demise as Helen is about everything else that goes on here.

"Listen," I begin, "do you mind if —"

He cuts me off to say, "Nope—do what ya gotta do, and take all the time you need. I'll still be here when you get back."

Something about the simple words reassure me.

As I get to my feet, I wrap up his burger and say, "I'll put this in your fridge. Maybe you'll want one of the nurses to reheat it later."

Dad nods. "Maybe." Unlike usual, he didn't even say it was good, and I almost got the impression he's lost the taste for it. But I can't worry about everything at once. *One step at a time; deal with what's directly before you.*

On my way out, Helen exits one of the resident's rooms in front of me. "You look like you're on your way to a fire," she observes.

"No, but something that feels almost as urgent," I tell her, striding past. Only then I stop and look back. "Hey Helen, could I borrow that Santa suit of yours?"

December 21

Lexi

Today is the last Saturday before Christmas, but already I feel the loss of the season. Because it's not the season itself I'm thinking of—it's my beloved little shop. The weather is bright and clear for a change, and yesterday we did well—but it wasn't nearly enough to make up for all the slow days, and I know today won't be, either. It's a near impossibility at this point.

As I flip the *Closed* sign to *Open* and turn the lock, I let out a sigh. Not only are there no hordes of eager shoppers waiting to bust down my door, there's also no Travis. I haven't seen him, for coffee or anything else, since our midnight kisses in the snowy street.

Has it been too much for him, all the Christmas stuff I shoved down his throat? It seemed like he was having fun, but I *was* kind of pushy at times— did it all ultimately re-Scroogify him?

Or...has it been too much *me*? I thought our kisses were amazing, but maybe they weren't as great for him? Or maybe he's realized I have real feelings for him and doesn't return them? And maybe that's for the best anyway because, as far as I know, despite the wish that disappeared from my pocket, he's still not planning to be in Winterberry long term.

Basically, I'm pretty dejected.

And Dara can see it from across the room where she's restocking rolls of wrapping paper. She knows everything that's been going on.

"Look at it this way," she tells me. "No matter what happens, with the shop, or with Travis, you've done some wonderful things to make a lot of people happy this holiday season. Nothing can change that. You've given a lot of people a far merrier Christmas than they'd have had without you and your wishing box and your giving heart."

Taking all that in, I walk across the old hardwood floor and pull her into a hug. Because she's right. No matter what I may lose in the coming days or weeks or months, she's reminded me of the good in the world—even if some of that good came from me. But much of it also came from Travis. And Helen and Dara and the choir.

"Listen," I say, pulling back to look at her. "If this is already the last hurrah for the Christmas Box, I've loved doing this with you and I'm grateful for your dedication and friendship."

"No, *you* listen," she says in reply. "This isn't over yet, so let's not go throwing in the towel. How many times have you told me we have to believe, and that miracles happen every day?"

Part of me wants to argue. I truly don't know what could happen to save the store at this late date in the holiday season. But then I glance above the shop's old mantelpiece, where the *Believe* sign still hangs. Surely I can make myself believe for just one more day. "Okay," I say, the reply quiet but earnest. "I'll try."

Then I deliver an overdue apology. "By the way, I'm so sorry I didn't think about how your mom would get up the stairs to Christmas dinner. And I'm also sorry that your wish wasn't left between you and the box. But when Travis saw it, he immediately offered to carry her up and said we shouldn't worry about it. I mean, as long as she's okay with that."

Dara tilts her head to ponder it. "Hmm, will she be okay with letting a big, strong, drop-dead gorgeous younger man use his muscles to carry little ole her up to your apartment? Yes, I think she'll survive." Then she drops the sarcasm to add, "And it's sweet of him. He's a good guy."

Words which float down through me to settle at my core. He *is* a good guy. No matter what happens between us in the end. And when I think back to the teenage bad boy I once suffered that ill-advised crush on, the fact that he turned out as he did seems pretty miraculous itself. Without that, all these wishes never would have been granted.

That's when the sleighbells announce the first shopper of the day, and I look up to see a woman I don't know, with two girls of around eight and ten tagging along behind her. "The Christmas Box! Where every day is Christmas!" she says, beaming as she recites to me the words painted on my front window. "What a lovely idea!"

A little thrown by her enthusiasm, despite that she kind of reminds me of myself—or who I was a month ago—I smile back at her. "Welcome! Look around and let us know if you need any help."

As she and her daughters shop, a few minutes later a thirty-something couple comes in—and the woman, in leggings and an oversize sweatshirt, seems just as entranced. "Oh, this is my kinda place! I've died and gone to heaven!"

Dara and I exchange what's-happening-here? smiles before she answers, "Well, we're glad you came by."

"We're on our way to my parents' house in Detroit for Christmas, and we've been on the road since five this morning," she explains, "but I insisted we stop."

"Yeah, we were gonna finish our gift-shopping once we got there," the slightly-rumpled-from-travel guy at her side tells us, "but looks like we might be doing it here."

"Oh yes," she says, "it's definitely happening here. Get out the credit card, honey."

And then...it keeps happening. More people keep coming in to the Christmas Box until we're jam-packed. And though I see a few locals, most seem to be from out of town.

I'm busy showing people the wishing box—which is, of course, charming them—and pointing them toward specific items they're seeking. "Do you have any holiday sweaters?" "Where are your gift bags?" "This reindeer plate is adorable, but I'd like to buy three Do you have more?"

Meanwhile, Dara is manning the checkout, and after I fetch the reindeer plates and finish helping someone at the cocoa bar, I see the line is backing up, so I start bagging items while she rings them up.

"Hi, I'm Taylor," a thirty-something redhead tells me, holding out her hand across the bar as Dara tallies up the ornaments she's buying. "I'm Helen's niece, from Sweetwater."

My eyes widen as I warmly shake her hand. "Oh—yes, she's told me so much about you over the years. It's nice to finally meet you."

She glances around the place to say, "You've done great with your shop here. The whole town, in fact, seems so much livelier than I remember."

I nod. "I only opened a month ago, but the rest of the town has been rebounding from hard times for a few years now."

"Well, you seem to have the most popular place on Main Street," she declares on a congratulatory laugh.

I start to protest, thinking: No, that's Winterburger, or maybe the bakery. But today, suddenly, perhaps I *do* have the town hotspot. And I'm still completely dumbfounded by it.

"I run a bake shop in Sweetwater," she goes on, "but the town is struggling." She ends on a more somber sigh.

Being well-acquainted with that kind of pain, I sympathize. But I also know what a little faith can bring—even just today it seems to have presented me with some inexplicable miracle—so I tell her, "My advice is to keep on believing. And hey, you should drop a wish for Sweetwater in our wishing box—you never know. Sometimes wishes come true."

"I'll do that," she says, then glances toward the door, which Helen has just walked through wearing a velour sweatsuit. "Ah, there's my sweet aunt. We're meeting up here, then having lunch before I head back home in a couple of hours."

I remind her to make that wish before she leaves, then wave to Helen before I get back to the business of business, which continues to boom.

And though I know Helen is the reason Taylor came in, Dara and I both remain stumped about the rest of them, so when an older woman mentions that she's on her way to Chattanooga, I finally ask the question. "Where did you hear about us?" A spontaneous laugh leaves me as I add, "We're trying to figure out where all these people are coming from."

"Oh, I saw the sign on the expressway," she says, "and the guy in the Santa suit."

I just blink. "You saw the what and the what?"

Travis

Talk about absurd, how-did-I-get-here-and-what-am-I-doing? moments. I can't believe I'm standing at the Winterberry I-75 off-ramp in a saggy Santa suit, ringing a bell that

Helen informed me she used "when I worked the Salvation Army kettle outside Lexi's grandma's diner."

But here I stand, waving people toward the Christmas Box after two crazy days of fevered preparation.

First, I called up Richard Hargis and told him about a business that needed immediate help, and my idea of putting a big sign on his property, facing the interstate. He told me what I already knew, that there were permits to get and hoops to jump through, and he wasn't sure it was legal, period, as close to the road as I was suggesting—but then he added on a laugh, "Imagine we could probably get away with it for a day or two, though."

Then I was so bold as to ask if he could help me build and erect it.

He answered with a big sigh. "Kinda busy with the holidays upon us, but...maybe my son can help. Gonna *need* help to make it big enough to read from the expressway."

Then I even went a step further, knowing I was already pushing my luck, and asked if he thought one or both of his kids would do the lettering on the sign.

When he hesitated, I added, "I'll handle whatever parts I can—I'll work on this around the clock if I need to—but I don't have that kind of talent, or the time to find anyone else."

"To be honest," Richard said over the phone, "this is turning into a pretty big ask."

"I'm aware," I told him. "And I apologize. But it's the only thing I can think of." Then I played that last card I was holding. "And...it's my dad's dying wish."

"That son of a gun," he said. "Sounds about like something he'd pull."

"Yep," I replied.

"Well," he said, after a little more hesitation, "I've seen the little shop up there in town, and I remember her grandma's business, and I know what it's like to have something you've worked at end up failing. Plus, if I say no, your dad might haunt me from the grave like a ghost of Christmas past. So you head on over to my place and we'll get started, and in the meantime, I'll call my kids and drag them into this harebrained scheme, too."

I thanked him, then spent the last two days working with his family on the sign. It's simple, but it shows up well with red lettering on a white background.

THE CHRISTMAS BOX
Where Every Day is Christmas
Gifts * Homegoods * Decorations
Exit Here. Turn Right. Then Left.

Of course, I dressed it up some, not only to be attention-grabbing, but because I'm planning to be out here until after dark. I hauled Dad's old generator from the farm, put floodlights in place, and used a tall ladder to help string big, old-fashioned Christmas bulbs around the edges. Then I bought an enormous inflatable waving snowman to tether to the ground next to one signpost.

It was awkward working with three people who clearly felt impinged upon, and I couldn't blame them—but as the project came together, their attitudes changed, similar to how mine did while granting wishes with Lexi. By the time their parts were done, they seemed downright cheerful, wishing me good luck with it.

It's almost two in the afternoon, and I can't believe how many cars have pulled off, waving and blinking their lights at the crazy guy running up and down the ramp in a Santa suit, some of them slowing down to ask me exactly where to go. I've been waiting for one of those cars to come with flashing blue lights on top because I'm sure this is all kinds of illegal, but so far, it's only been friendly shoppers who apparently like the idea of a Christmas store more than I ever could have suspected when I first walked in the place.

My truck sits parked in a gravel area at the end of the ramp, and when I see a sedan pull over next to it and someone waving at me from a distance, I jog in that direction—to find Helen getting out. She's wearing some kind of plush sweatsuit instead of her usual scrubs. "Take off that suit and let me have it," she says by way of greeting.

"Um, what?" I squint my confusion.

"I'm giving you a break," she says. "Go get yourself some lunch. Visit with your pop for an hour or two."

"Helen, that's sweet, but it's cold out here, and the cops might come rolling up to run me off at any second."

"I'm not averse to a little cold," she tells me. "And if they show up, maybe I'll just run faster." She ends on a laugh.

"Helen," I scold her. "I can't let you do that."

"Why not?" she argues. "Besides, I know most of the po-po in these parts, and I'll probably fend for myself better with them than you would anyway. Now c'mon.

Off with the beard. Off with the coat. I just had lunch with my niece and finished my holiday shopping, and now I can't think of anything I'd rather do on my day off than run around in a Santa suit waving folks to my girl's shop."

So, right there next to the exit ramp, I shed the Santa suit from over my athletic pants and sweatshirt, then help Helen into it, handing off the bell like a baton in a relay race. After which I hop back in the truck, heading to town just long enough to grab a quick slice of pizza for lunch before rushing to the manor.

But as I pass back through, a glance at the Christmas Box shows me that—like magic—it's filled with people. Like *Christmas* magic, as Lexi's always talking about. I guess she's right that sometimes the magic comes from someone's actions, someone's care.

I don't stop, but the vision of all those people inside stays with me, making me feel the same way I did after we snuck to Mikayla's house, after we installed a wheelchair ramp, after we hauled that giant tree to the nursing home. Except I feel it even more this time.

Dad's sleeping when I arrive, but when he wakes up, he's glad to see me and enjoys hearing my tales from the last two days.

"You tell ole Rich I appreciate him coming through like that."

"I will," I promise.

I check the fridge to see that the last burger I brought him is still there and offer to get it heated up, but he declines. "Maybe later. Ain't hungry."

"You gotta eat, Dad," I insist. "Gotta keep your strength up."

"For what?" he asks me, chuckling. "Ain't planning on running any marathons anytime soon. Now you best get back and rescue Helen I'm pretty tired—might just fall back asleep here shortly."

When I get back to the exit ramp, I find Santa Helen dancing on the roadside to Wham's "Last Christmas," which blares from her pocket. I can see people in cars coming off the exit smiling and laughing. I almost hate to interrupt her, because she's better at this than me—but I jog up anyway, announcing my return. "Time for you to get in from the cold, lady."

"Already?" she asks through the flowing white beard. "I'll tell ya what, Trav—this was fun!"

For me, as I put the suit back on and send Helen on her way, it's *not* fun. It's cold and exhausting, and I feel silly as hell. But I'd do it all night if it helps the Christmas Box stay open.

When darkness falls, I pull out a battery-charged flood light and shine it on myself. That's how dedicated I am.

But by the time the clock strikes seven-forty-five, fifteen minutes before Lexi's closing time on this last Saturday before Christmas, I'm well-ready to pack up my light, get in my truck, and blast the heat while I shed the Santa suit from over my more low-key clothing. Although I can't see the big sign from where I am, Richard offered to drive out and turn off the lights a few minutes before eight, and later I'll head there myself to dig out the posts to let it lay flat on the ground since its one day of tempting legal fate has passed. As for what happens to the sign after that, Richard said, "Eh, let's talk about that after Christmas, huh? Might need it next year." He ended with a wink.

On the way back to town, I give him a call and thank him again for all the help, and I pass along Dad's thanks, too. He sounds happy enough about the whole thing, and wishes me a merry Christmas.

I'm beyond exhausted, and hungry, and more than ready to crash with my dog for a little while before I go dig up a sign under the cover of darkness, but when I pull to the curb across from the Christmas Box to see the lights still on, I can't resist going over.

I can tell through the glass that the place is a mess. Lexi is scurrying around, trying to put things back in order, when the bells on the door draw her gaze my way.

I give her a grin. "Looks like the same tornado that took down that gingerbread house of yours came barreling through your shop here. Busy day?"

"You could say that. *Banner* day, in fact." She looks as tired as I feel, but that doesn't keep a grateful smile from unfurling across her face.

I decide to play dumb. "Yeah? How banner?"

"Like...I-think-I'm-solvent banner. Like I-had-to-restock-things-all-day banner. Any idea how that happened?" she asks, head tilting and voice filled with playful suspicion.

The Christmas Box

"Oh," I say, confessing just a little, "I guess it's possible I had a hand in getting the word out to holiday travelers."

"Is it true you actually put on a Santa suit and waved people in from the expressway, man who hates Christmas?"

I shrug, offer up one more small grin, and make another, *bigger* confession. "I must like *you* more than I hate Christmas."

"I don't really think you hate Christmas anymore," she accuses me.

Too tired to *completely* give up my Scroogy reputation tonight, I just tell her, "Don't get started making crazy accusations, Alexandra Louise."

"My only regret about having so many customers today," she tells me, "is that I was too busy to come see for myself the day Travis Hutchins paraded around in a Santa suit next to the interstate."

I just laugh, still not quite able to believe I did it. "Never happened," I joke. "I'll deny it 'til my dying day."

"So I was wondering," she says, flashing wide eyes, sounding a little flirtatious, and making me remember those kisses we shared, "if you might let me thank you."

Well, this sounds promising. "What did you have in mind?"

"Are you busy the night of Christmas Eve?"

"Well, you know us Grinches don't make a lot of holiday plans, so I'm free as a partridge in a pear tree."

I feel her pretty laughter wash over me. "Then maybe you could come over. We could snack on some Christmas cookies. I could torture you with a Christmas movie or two. And after that...who knows?"

Okay, I'm liking the sound of this. Especially the last part. "It's a date," I say. And yeah, I've tried like hell to resist her charms, but...my resolve has worn thin. Maybe seeing where this thing between us leads is just another way of taking one day, one step, at a time.

That's when the business phone behind the counter rings. I've never actually heard it do that before, and we both look at it like it just sprouted antlers.

"You should get that," I tell her.

As she answers, I walk to the end of the bar to see a little hot chocolate remaining in the cocoa machine. Still trying to warm up, I reach over to grab a mug, and my cell phone falls from my pocket, *clunking* to the floor.

I bend to grab it, hit a button to make sure it still works, and then...notice something *else* on the floor peeking from between the short legs of a wicker stand where Lexi keeps extra cocoa toppings and paper cups. I recognize it almost immediately as one of the wish slips, and pluck it up, figuring it belongs in the box, that it must have gotten dropped when we were looking through them all.

She's telling someone to hold on and that she'll check in the back—when I see that it's not just any wish. It's from *her*.

Name: Lexi
My wish: That Travis decides to stay in town, and maybe he even falls in love with me.

That's when she exits the back room, telling the person

on the phone, "Yes, I found one more and we're open tomorrow from noon to eight."

I cram the wish in my pants pocket.

I'm shaken, though, unsure how to feel.

When I was concerned she might want something serious with me, it made me pull back. And even if I've decided to quit worrying about that so much...this is *big*.

But one day at a time, right? *Worry about the steps in front of you today, not the whole journey.* It's the only response I can muster right now, even after what I just read. And it's not like I have to *do* something about her wish. Sure, I've gotten into the wish-granting business lately, but this one I can let ride.

When she hangs up, she turns to face me with, "Have you eaten? I'm starved. I could whip something up at my place."

"Thanks," I tell her, "but I have to run. I have to take down a big sign near the expressway before morning." I wonder if I look ill-at-ease. Since I suddenly kind of am.

Her eyes widen. "It's that urgent?"

"Actually, yeah. Because it's a little bit illegal." I'm holding my thumb and index finger close together. "A rogue Santa's work is never done."

Appearing surprised and now mildly worried, she begins shooing me. "Then go. Get moving." Then her eyes widen. "But do you need help? Because I can go with you."

"Nope, I've got it all under control," I assure her, heading for the door, unexpectedly glad to be leaving.

As I reach it, though, she stops me with, "Travis."

I look over my shoulder to see her walking toward me.

And before I know what's happening, she lifts one hand to my cheek and plants a soft, warm kiss on the other. It moves all through me.

"Thank you, again," she says. "You literally saved Christmas. Or the Christmas Box anyway. I'm so used to being on my own, and...well, no one's ever done anything like this for me before. I'll never forget what you did today."

December 22

Travis

The next morning I sleep late. I deserve it.

When I finally open my eyes, I find a scruffy white dog standing on the bed staring down at me.

"What?" I say. "A guy can't sleep in after a hard night's work? I bet you don't see Santa's dog giving *him* that kind of look on Christmas morning." Then she paws at my arm, and I understand. "Oh, I get it. It's past the princess's breakfast hour. Looks like I've spoiled you in record time."

But then I reach out and run my hand through her fur, scratching the way I know she likes. "I think Lexi's in love with me," I say without segue.

She doesn't answer, of course.

But me, I keep going, apparently needing to get some stuff off my chest. "She wants me to stay here. She wants...

well, what most people want, I guess. And she's a great girl. And this place is...better than I remember.

I let out a sigh. "Still, there's a lot being thrown at me fast here, you know? I have you to worry about now, and Dad to worry about, and...I came here not feeling responsible for anybody but myself. How much is one guy supposed to take on over the course of a single December?"

That's when my phone buzzes on the bedside table and I grab it to look. Helen's calling.

"Hey, Helen," I answer, tired but pleasant. "Thanks again for your help yesterday. Lexi thinks the shop will be fine now, so the hard work paid off."

"I'm so glad to hear that," she says, "but that's not why I'm calling." She sounds tense.

I hesitate, bracing myself, before asking, "What's up?"

She hesitates, too. "It's your dad, Travis. He's stopped eating altogether since the day before yesterday. When that happens, it's the body's way of beginning to shut down."

All the blood drains from my face as the harsh reality I've been dreading these past couple of weeks hits hard. "So this is it?"

"There's no telling how long," she says. "It could be a day, it could be a week. But you should come."

I get up, take a shower, get dressed. I feed the dog and change her puppy pad. I take my time, moving methodically around the apartment. Maybe I'm just distracting myself. Maybe I'm taking a last few moments of normalcy and peace before whatever happens next.

As I step out into the cold, headed to the truck, I make a detour. Maybe it's more putting-off-the-inevitable, but on a lark I cross the street to the Christmas Box. As the sleighbells announce my arrival, I question the decision, but it's too late.

Lexi looks up to greet me from behind the counter. "Good morning." Her smile fills me with warmth, despite the cold outside, despite where I'm about to go. But at the same time, it tightens my chest. Because of that wish she made.

"Morning," I say. No smile from me—I'm too stressed.

"Coffee?" She sounds happy to see me. Normally, I've come to like that. Today, though, every feeling inside me is twisted up into a confusing knot.

"No," I say. "Can't stay. Have to get to the manor. Helen called. Said it might not be long now."

Stunned compassion fills her gaze. "Travis, I'm so sorry."

"Knew it was coming," I say woodenly. I realize I probably sound like the guy who walked in here almost a month ago. A little on the grumpy side, and bitter. I haven't felt those things in a while, but apparently they're still there, lurking just beneath the surface. Maybe they just got covered up in layers of Christmas wrapping and snow and other things I can't quite put my finger on.

"Still," she says. "Things have changed between you and him, and even if they hadn't, such big losses are hard. Take it from me, I know."

She does. I just don't have her grace when it comes to dealing with things like this. So I move ahead with why I crossed the street. "Do you have any little stuffed animals?" I hold up my hands to indicate the size I'm seeking, not more than four or five inches tall.

She looks understandably perplexed by the request, but leaves her spot behind the bar as she says, "Over here."

She leads me to a table with a small selection of tiny plush toys, and I pluck up a stuffed gray kitten wearing a Santa hat. "This'll do."

She's eyeing me peculiarly, and as we walk to the checkout, she says, "If this is for Marley, it might be better to get her a proper dog toy."

I press my lips together, for some reason reluctant to explain, but then I do anyway. "Remember Shannon from the manor? She collects little stuffed animals."

I'm not looking at her as I talk—I'm pulling out my wallet—but I feel that smile again just the same. Yesterday I loved that smile. Today I'm still overwhelmed by knowing how Lexi feels about me. And by knowing this thing I came here for is finally happening: My father is really about to die.

"That's very sweet of you," she tells me.

Instead of replying to that, I say, "If I get hung up at the manor over the next day or two, could you feed the dog?" It's just occurred to me that I'm not sure what to expect and I've somehow become responsible for keeping another living thing alive.

"Of course," she says. "Just text me if you're not coming home."

"Thanks," I say, picking up the little red bag she just topped off with candy-cane-striped tissue paper—and then I'm gone, out the door.

Not my finest moment. But I know she understands.

Well, at least when it comes to the part she knows about: my dad. As for the part she *doesn't* know about, me finding her wish...I haven't gotten to digest it yet, and I suddenly have more pressing things on my mind. Death and dying, for instance.

I drive to the manor on auto-pilot, and I stay that way as I move up the hall, weaving between wheelchairs. I'm forced to be more present, though, as I step up to Shannon's open door and knock on it, peeking in to see her sitting by the window, probably watching her birds.

She looks up as I approach, and I hold out the bag. "I got this for you."

Taking it, she reaches inside to pull out the stuffed cat. Her face doesn't change, and at first I feel a little stupid to have possibly picked something she doesn't like. But then her eyes turn glassy, and I realize that maybe her face *can't* change, and that her *eyes* are telling me how she feels. She's clearly working hard to enunciate as she grabs onto my hand, tight. "This is very nice. Very nice. Thank you."

I give a short nod and tell her, "You have a merry Christmas if I don't see you before then."

There I go, wishing someone a merry Christmas again. But I can't examine stuff like that right now—instead I have to go face a reality I'm not ready for.

Mostly, he sleeps. He's entered hospice care, just hours ago, which Helen informed me is necessary for the increased level of pain medication to keep him comfortable now.

I sit next to his bed, wondering if I'll ever hear his voice again or if he's said his last words—when he opens his eyes and rasps, "Water."

There's a cup with a straw in it on the table, so I hold it down for him to drink from. "I'm here, Dad," I tell him.

And I am. The dread, the fear, the wall that seemed to be rising up inside me before I got here...it all takes a backseat now to doing whatever I can for him. Which isn't much. But I can be here.

Christmas Eve

Lexi

The shop is quiet. Most people have holiday gatherings, but I don't, so I've opened and will stay that way until six, for anyone's last minute needs.

Dara is with her family, driving her mom to her sister's house in Louisville. Sometimes I envy Dara for getting all this time with her mother, the kind I didn't get to have—I left for college assuming, as anyone would, that I'd have countless more years with her. But now I wonder if it's harder to lose one's parent suddenly, without warning, as I did, or if it's more difficult to watch them slowly fade.

For Travis's dad, it's just a matter of waiting now. I've been feeding the dog and keeping her company—and feeling sad about what Travis is going through. When I texted him my support, he replied with something more...

well, *honest* than I'm used to from him when talking about his dad: *I should have been here long before I was. Years ago.*

My heart breaks for him. I texted back: *You have nothing to feel bad about.* They had a fraught relationship and Travis felt driven away—that wasn't his fault. And he didn't know that Tom became a kinder, gentler man with age. That wasn't his fault either.

As the day passes, I'm surprised with more shoppers than I expected, and everyone's moods are so festive that it cheers me up.

A neighbor of Mikayla's even mentions that the Watkins kids are having a much better holiday than expected "because some good Samaritan left a tree and presents on her porch! I haven't seen her this happy since Danny flew the coop."

"How wonderful!" I say, elated to hear our gesture was well-received.

Soon after that, Nick from Winterburger steps through the door, bundled up in coat, scarf, and gloves, toting a small bag from the Country Creamery next door. "Merry Christmas, Lexi!"

"Merry Christmas to you, too. Peppermint ice cream?" I ask, pointing to the sack. It's Carl's flavor of the month each December.

He nods, flashing a big smile. "Goes great with Linda's chocolate cake. Speaking of which, she says you're holding a serving bowl for her."

"Ah, yes," I say. "It's wrapped up behind the counter, and she already paid over the phone."

"You oughta see Carl today," he tells me, seeming

uncharacteristically chatty. "The man's downright chipper. Until just now, I didn't even know he could smile. Was bragging he bought Gina a diamond bracelet for their anniversary and looking proud as a peacock."

It's all I can do not to gasp. "You don't say." As I pass him the bag, I observe out loud, "Seems like you're in the Christmas spirit, too, Nick." He's usually a pretty low-key guy.

"You better believe it," he confirms. "Cash is finally going to ask Marissa to marry him—at our family gathering tonight! It's gonna be a very good Christmas for us!"

This time, I do gasp with joy. "Nick, that's such great news!"

"Tell Travis I said thanks, by the way."

"For...?" I prod.

He gives his head a short, uncertain shake. "We had a weird conversation last week that led me to sit Cash down and have a heart-to-heart. Next thing I know, Cash tells me he's ready to step up and be the man Marissa needs him to be. And between me and you, it's about time. His mother and I are over the moon."

So yet another wish successfully granted, all because Travis did his part in one I'd somehow forgotten about along the way.

And then, still more Christmas magic happens. Other people stop in to tell me their wishes came true!

"Lexi, I couldn't believe it when my son walked through the door—he originally had to work through the holidays, but I put a wish in your box that he could come home, and he showed up on my doorstep this morning!"

241

"My mother got the word that her scans came back clear! That's what I wished for, in the pretty box—for my mom to be cancer-free, and it happened!"

"Lexi, my husband surprised me with a new car. Well, a used car. But our old clunker was barely hanging on, and money's tight these days, so I had no idea what we were gonna do. A fella Bob knows was selling this real nice SUV at a good price because he needed the money before Christmas. And it's exactly what I asked for in the box."

And finally comes Greg, a big smile plastered across his face. "Your little box made a dream come true, Lex. Tony agreed to look into adoption. He even brought it up himself! I can't imagine a better Christmas gift."

I remember Janet's wish for a new car—one of the many Travis and I set aside in lieu of those we could more easily deliver. But as for Marla's mother and Kim's son, those are wishes I never saw—they must have come in later. And as for Greg, I totally dropped the ball on that one—I missed Tony's UPS deliveries with so much going on.

But they all came true anyway!

And my wish for the shop came true, too, with Travis's help.

Which can only mean...the wishing box really *is* kind of magic!

Even if Travis just speedily built it in his father's workshop. Even if some of the wishes needed a little help from us.

As I stand there in the stillness of the shop after everyone's gone, listening to Michael Buble dream of a white Christmas, my head is spinning. Both in joy for everyone whose wish came true...and in a bit of more self-centered speculation.

The one wish I know of that *hasn't* come true is my own, the one that went missing. Will it happen now, as well? What Travis did for me the other day was incredible—but it doesn't mean he's staying. And it doesn't mean he's in love with me, either.

Maybe it's too much to hope for. Maybe you should just be grateful for all the other wishes coming true. So many people are having merry Christmases. And your shop is safe — your family legacy remains alive and well in Winterberry. That should mean everything.

Unfortunately, though, somewhere along the way, *he* started mattering, too.

As a sinking feeling comes over me at the thought, my eyes fall on the sign above the mantel across the room. *Believe.* It's the last thing I saw before shoppers filled the store on Saturday. So I focus on it again now.

That's when I glance outside to see...snow. Thick, heavy snowflakes are falling fast. Okay, I love a white Christmas, but this has gotten ridiculous. Even Mr. Buble's wish is being granted.

Checking my weather app, it looks like heavy snow is falling all across the Midwest. Good for Santa, bad for people's holiday travel plans. But me, I'm safe and sound, just waiting for one more wish to come true.

Travis

It's been a long couple of days at Dad's side. I've slept in the reclining chair next to his bed and have been eating the cafeteria food, whatever's on the menu.

Dad sleeps more than he's awake. And when he's awake, sometimes he's lucid and other times he's not. Yesterday around lunchtime, he opened his eyes and said, "You still here? You should go home and get some sleep, come back in the morning."

I mustered a small smile to inform him, gently, "It *is* morning."

Without looking very surprised, he murmured, "Hmm."

When I told Helen I find it hard to watch him waste away from not eating, she simply replied, "It's the way of things. The natural order of the body closing up shop."

Helen says if nothing changes, I should keep my plans with Lexi tonight. And that I should go to Christmas dinner at her place tomorrow with their group of "misfit toys," as Helen called them. She pointed out that I need some breaks, and she's probably right.

When I got here two days ago, I was nervous about that wish of Lexi's—and maybe I still am. Does it bother me, worry me, make me feel pressured? Again, maybe. But at the very same time, right now being with her sounds like the safest place in the world.

Looking back to the bed, I wonder if Dad knows he's dying, that this is it, the end of everything for him. If he somehow thinks this is just a setback, I'm not going to disabuse him of the notion.

Next to me, he stirs a little. Then he opens his eyes, his gaze connecting with mine. "Is your mother here?"

This is where things get tricky. Should I lie? I hardly ever lie. I lied a lot as a teenager—a result of poor parenting and trying to stay out of trouble—and I decided it was a bad way to live as an adult. But he clearly never stopped loving her, and he wants to believe that she's come to be with him in this moment, or that she's been here all along. So I lie.

"She just stepped out of the room," I say, making this up as I go. "But says to tell you she loves you."

"Hmm. Funny. Always seemed so mad at me," he muses, lying on his side, appearing frail and weak. "But I love her, too." Then he closes his eyes again.

For the first time, I begin to wonder how often he thinks of her. Frequently, or just now because it's the end? I haven't heard from her since she disappeared one day while I was at school during my sophomore year. She packed some bags and took the car. That was it, not even a note to say goodbye. I have no idea if she's alive or dead. Nor do I care.

But wait. I've learned a few things these past few weeks. PI didn't think I cared about my dad, either, but turns out love and hate are just different sides of the same coin. I guess that kind of abandonment leaves a wound that never really heals.

And then something else hits me for the first time ever. Dad was an awful father there for a while, but...at least he stayed. He stayed. And maybe *that's* why I'm here right now.

The hospice lady comes in around four that afternoon to check his vital signs. When he stirs and moans slightly, she administers morphine from a dropper onto his tongue. After that, she whispers with Helen in a corner, then gives me a somber nod before leaving the room.

Helen's voice comes softly as she walks over to lay a hand on my shoulder. "There's been a change, Travis. He's starting to fade. His heart's beating slower. Probably won't be long now."

A few minutes later, my phone buzzes in my pocket, and I pull it out to find a text from Lexi: *Just wanted you to know that Cash is proposing to Marissa tonight, thanks to your conversation with Nick. And there are other wishes coming true from the box that we didn't even have a hand in! S as far as I'm concerned, it really IS a wishing box.*

Despite myself, it makes me smile. Do I really think that box is magic? Nope. But am I starting to believe in miracles? Maybe. I message her back. *That's crazy. But great.*

How's your dad doing? she asks.

No miracle for him, though, which makes the whole thing hard to understand—why do some people get miracles and others don't? I don't rain on her miracle parade, though. I just keep it simple. *Might be a long night. Helen thinks he'll go any time now. Sorry I have to cancel.*

I understand, she texts back a minute later. *And I'm here if you need me.*

This is something I have to do by myself, but she makes me feel a little less alone.

A few hours later, darkness has long since fallen outside the window in Dad's room, I've eaten a tray of ham, green beans, mashed potatoes, and cornbread for dinner in the recliner, and I'm using the remote to flip around on TV. I stop when I see Jimmy Stewart in black-and-white and know I've stumbled upon "It's a Wonderful Life". For some reason, it nearly makes my heart skip a beat. Maybe because I haven't watched it since I was a kid. Part of hating Christmas after Mom left, I guess. Now it brings back memories I'd rather face than keep running from.

I'm not sure how long I've been watching in the dimly-lit room when dad asks, "Is that 'It's a Wonderful Life'?"

I flinch, then flick my gaze to him. I honestly thought I'd never hear his voice again. And this time he even got it right about the movie. "Um, yeah," I answer, completely thrown.

On the screen, Mary's singing about buffalo girls, and George is trying to deny his feelings for her.

"I like this part," Dad says.

"Me, too." The part where George begins to figure out that life can be great even if it's not turning out the way he expected. But I'm still dumbfounded by Dad's sudden alertness. Despite short exchanges with him over the last two days, clarity has been lacking.

"Can you sit me up?"

I barely know what to make of the request—it almost feels like I'm dreaming—but I reach for the controls, raising the back of the hospital bed until he's upright enough to see.

We keep watching together, but my attention is split between the movie and my astonishment that Dad is suddenly awake, despite the morphine, and glued to the screen. How can this be?

Just as it goes to a commercial, Helen peeks in, and I dart my gaze over in time to see her eyes go wide. "Look who woke up!" she says by way of addressing Dad. She and I share glances of surprise.

"Watching my favorite holiday movie with my boy here," Dad tells her as cheerfully as he would have a week ago.

"That's wonderful," she says. "Want me to make some popcorn?" She tosses a wink in my direction.

Dad just laughs. "Maybe later. Not hungry right now." Again, he says this like a man who didn't stop eating three days ago.

I get up from my chair, tell Dad I'll be right back, and step out into the hallway to speak with Helen. "What's happening here?" I ask.

But she simply holds her hands out, palms up. And though she's surprised, she's clearly not as surprised as me. "I've told you before, these things are hard to predict. I've seen crazier occurrences, believe it or not. Sometimes they're just not quite ready to say goodbye, and they linger for longer than any medical professional can understand.

Sometimes lingering even turns into rebounding for a while."

I let out a long sigh, thoroughly confused. "So you have no idea what will happen now," I say to clarify.

"Sorry," she tells me, "but not really."

In one way, I'm happy—he's not gone yet. But I'm also worn out by riding an emotional rollercoaster. I run a hand back through my hair, wishing...I don't even know what. That I was somewhere else? That the mother who deserted us fifteen years ago was here with me through this, like she should have been? That life wasn't so damn complicated?

"Listen," Helen says, "know what I think? You've been here around the clock for two days and you're exhausted. Like I said, you need a break. Why don't you keep your plans with Lexi, after all. After you finish the movie with your pop, that is." She gives me another wink, I guess because she's delighted by this sudden change in Dad—but I'm still not feeling quite as merry. My emotions are shredded at this point.

"Are you sure?"

She nods. "Take an hour or two. I can call you with any changes."

As I ease my tired body back into the recliner, I send Lexi a text. *Crazy thing. He's suddenly rebounding. We're actually watching "It's a Wonderful Life."*

She answers quickly. *Really? That's amazing!*

Helen said maybe he just wasn't quite ready to go yet, that things can change, I text back. *Be there after the movie.*

I'm still not ready to think about Lexi's wish. Could I stay here? Could I be with her in the way she wants? These remain questions too big for me to handle right now. But the idea of seeing her tonight—maybe snuggling up with her next to the Christmas tree—sounds...well, like the best end to this day I can imagine.

After the movie comes back on, Dad says, "It's nice getting to watch this with you again. Like old times. Better times." Then he surprises me even further by reaching out for my hand.

His touch is warm even if his grip is almost non-existent. It makes me sad all over again that this man who not so long ago swung a hammer with this same hand can now barely grasp mine. And I don't ever remember a time when we held hands, father and son, other than out of practicality —him not wanting to lose his little kid in a crowd at the county fair or to keep me from running out in front of a car in a busy parking lot. But if he wants to hold my hand *now*, it's okay with me.

Not long after George Bailey jumps off a bridge into icy water, only to be rescued by a second-class angel, the movie goes to commercial again, and though he's been silent a while now, Dad says quietly, "I wasn't there when you needed me, back when you were just a boy. Nothing was your fault if I ever made you feel that way. Wish I'd had the strength to do things different, better. I always loved you, though. Still do."

I'm speechless for a second—I didn't see this coming. I'd long since given up on it, in fact. And now, I almost wish he hadn't brought it up, because a few sentences doesn't fix years of mistakes that drove me away.

But the words that instantly spill out of me are, "It's

okay, Dad. It's okay." Partly because a lot of forgiveness has come these last few weeks. And partly because, my conscience tells me that when a man is dying, you absolve him so he can move on in peace. You just do. You let things go, no matter how big, no matter how much you never thought you would. "I love you, too." We weren't people who said 'I love you' a lot, but it's good we're saying it now.

He manages to squeeze my hand, just a little, and the look on his face is one of peace.

We watch the rest of the movie in silence and I'm drawn back in to the uplifting story I haven't seen in so many years. Same as when I was a kid and would lie on the couch watching the story unfold, Mom and Dad in their easy chairs nearby, my heart swells at the end when George finds out how many people love him.

As the credits roll, I say to Dad, "Well, looks like Clarence got his wings again and George is still the richest guy in town."

I glance over—only his eyes are shut now, and an odd sort of breath leaves him, and it's his last. I can't explain how I know this, but I do. He's gone.

Emotion floods me as I sit there gaping at him. Because death suddenly doesn't make sense to me. We all know about death. Logically, we get it. But when it happens right in front of your eyes, it's harder to comprehend. He was right here, talking to me, just minutes ago. Where is he now?

But then I remember I'm supposed to go get one of the nurses. I rush from the room and find Helen at the nurse's station. "He's gone."

She looks up, clearly as surprised as she was a couple of hours ago when he was suddenly awake, then grabs a stethoscope and starts toward his room. I follow but keep my distance as she feels for a pulse, then bends over him, pressing the stethoscope to his heart while she watches a clock on the wall.

It's a long, strange minute as the clock's second hand turns, and when finally she says, "Time of death, ten-oh-two," I let out a heavy sigh and I feel like I can't breathe. I need to get out of the room.

Leaving, I literally bump into Gabbi, who's walking an elderly woman up the hall, holding her arm to steady her.

"Sorry," I say.

She can see it in my face. "Oh—is he...?"

I just nod. I'm out of words.

"I'm so sorry, Travis," she tells me, pulling me into a tight, warm hug.

I barely know her, but I let her, my thoughts swirling, my heart reeling.

Yet that's when I feel something against my butt, and I begin to realize the old woman with Gabbi is taking my cell phone from my back pocket.

I pull free from the hug and snatch the phone back—not as nicely as I could, but damn, she caught me at a bad moment. And no matter how hard I've worked to be nice and understanding to the residents here, it's still a hard place to be. And the person I was here for all this time is dead. I don't have to be here anymore. And I don't *want* to be here anymore. So what am I waiting for?

Just like that, I start for the door. Helen can do the rest.

I know what happens now—she calls the funeral home and they come and get him, that simple. I'm done. Because suddenly this is all...Just. Too. Much. The world doesn't make sense.

Has it ever, for me? Up, down, up, down. Love, hate, leaving, rebuilding. And then these past few weeks...love again.

Damn, that's the last thing I expected. Love. And now he's gone.

Why bother loving someone if they're just gonna leave you? This time it wasn't Dad's fault—it was no one's fault—but he's still gone, and I'm left holding the bag of experiencing that strange, awful void.

As I emerge through the front doors and the cold air hits my face, it feels like escape. Like freedom.

Like I don't have to care anymore, or worry anymore.

Of course, I do still care. Something inside me is breaking. Why did I have to let myself get attached to him again these last few weeks? What was I thinking? I mean, I already know what comes from trusting in relationships. You end up alone. Every. Single. Time. In one way or another, everyone always leaves.

Snow falls thick and heavy, but I barely register the wetness on my face as I trudge through several fresh inches to my truck. It's covered in deep snow, too, but I get in, start it, use the wipers to clear the windshield. I crank up the heat, then pull my phone out and call Wally.

It goes to voicemail. Great. One more person who can't be counted on when I need him. Guess he's having a festive Christmas Eve with Edie and their kids—my cousins probably flew to Florida for the holiday. Well, merry freaking Christmas to your big, happy family.

I leave a message. "Dad's dead. I did my duty, and now I'm gone, outta here, back to my real life."

Lexi

Outside, a heavy blanket of white piles up on Main Street, but in my apartment, a fire crackles at the small hearth across the room. I sit on the couch in my coziest red sweater, Crinkle Bear perched next to me as we await our visitor.

I have mugs ready for hot chocolate, and a tray of cookies from the bakery rests on the coffee table next to a pine-scented candle. Beside the fireplace, my Christmas tree gives off a happy glow. And inside, I *feel* a happy glow.

I can't believe Travis's father actually rebounded! And I know the end will still come soon, but if he makes it through Christmas...well, that's just one more reason for Travis not to hate it anymore.

And from a selfish standpoint, I'm excited he's keeping our date. I understood when he had to cancel, but...well, the truth is that Christmas Eve can be a little lonely for me.

People would probably be surprised to know that. Clearly, it's not the vibe I give off. But when you don't have any close family, the days right around the holiday can be hard.

That's why I started our Christmas dinner for people who don't have anywhere else to go. It gave Christmas Day renewed purpose for me.

Which leaves Christmas Eve, a time when so many people gather with their loved ones as well. And I've never told my friends I find it a lonely night because I don't want anyone feeling sorry for me or as if they need to invite me to their family gatherings.

But finally *I* have someone to spend Christmas Eve with, too, and I can't wait to see him.

It's almost ten-thirty when I hear the familiar rumble of his truck pull to the curb outside.

Turning toward the window, I draw back a curtain and peek out. Wow, it's really coming down out there. Being a big night for holiday get-togethers, there are ample tire tracks through the snow, but it looks just as blizzard-like as when we delivered the tree to Bluegrass Manor.

I watch as Travis gets out and tromps through the snowfall into the Lucas Building. He probably wants to check on Marley before coming over, or maybe he wants to take a shower and change—he's had a long stay at the nursing home.

Upstairs, a light comes on, and I think maybe he'll plug in the tree—but he doesn't.

Okay, drop the curtain. You're not a smitten schoolgirl anymore—you don't need to spy on his every move.

No, you're a smitten woman, *excited about a date that's been a dozen years in the making.*

So as I get up to make the hot chocolate, I forgive myself the staring-out-the-window indulgence. After I start some milk heating in a pan on the stove, I pad back to the couch in my snowman socks, allowing myself one more anticipatory peek outside.

That's when Travis exits the building and...it's dark, but what am I seeing? I squint, looking harder, to find that his arms are full. He's carrying Marley and...a large duffel bag? Opening the passenger side door of his truck, he loads both inside.

Then he walks around the pickup in the heavily-falling snow, gets in, starts the engine, and races away from the curb, the truck fishtailing up Main Street before his taillights disappear.

I sit there staring at the empty street for a long moment. Did that really just happen? Did Travis Hutchins just pack up his dog and his belongings and leave town without a word? What about his Dad? Did he leave Tom behind after all of this? Or...maybe Tom's rebound was short-lived and he passed away tonight, after all.

And even if so, what about...me? I don't know what he and I have become, but it was...something. And I deserve better. Just like I did in high school.

Just where is it he thinks he's going in this weather? I know the old Ford is good in the snow, but according to the news, roads are hazardous all over the Midwest. If he thinks he's headed to Chicago tonight...I just shake my head. It's over five hours away on a sunny, perfect-weather day—and these are no conditions for travel.

As I curl up in a ball on the couch, my mind is a blurred mix of confusion, worry, and heartbreak. I'm forced to remember the man I first met downstairs on the day after Thanksgiving—slightly churlish, slightly bitter, and he hated Christmas. I thought my wishes had really changed him, changed *everything*, but I guess wanting him to stay just went too far. Or maybe I'm naïve and wishes don't really come true at all.

As my stomach ties into knots of rejection, I pull Crinkle into my arms, hugging him tight as I murmur, "Well, he stood me up again. Looks like it's just me and you again for another Christmas Eve. Why was I foolish enough to expect anything else?"

Travis

My truck sits alongside a desolate highway in a snowstorm somewhere in Indiana, out of gas.

I bang my hand on the steering wheel, and the dog flinches. "Sorry," I tell her.

I'm sorry for a lot of things right about now.

I'm sorry I roared away from Winterberry in too much of a frenzy to even notice the gas gauge the whole time I was driving. I'm sorry the snow hasn't let up since I left and the expressway is as empty as a frozen tundra. I'm sorry I can't reassure the faithful pup at my side that everything's going to be okay, because it's getting cold in the truck and we're miles between exits, with no lights in any direction. I'm sorry I pulled out my phone to dial 9-1-1 only to discover I let the battery go dead sometime between the moment Dad died and now. "I've made a colossal mess out of things," I glance toward the dog to say.

I'm also sorry my father is dead. I'm sorry I stayed away for so many years and didn't know this version of him longer. I realize I had good reason to leave—but we could have rebuilt our relationship long before now and that's squandered time I can never get back.

I'm sorry I felt so overwhelmed by all of that in the few minutes after he died. It still feels like there's been a hole ripped in my chest, but I can see more clearly now. "Where did I think I was rushing off to and why?" I ask Marley, as if I think she has the answers. "What is it I was trying so hard to get away from?"

The dog still doesn't reply, of course, but I dig a little deeper inside myself.

The answer to the first question: Safety maybe? But I'm not sure that really exists in any lasting way. And the answer to the second: Regret. And fear. And feelings. So many feelings, flooding me this past month.

If I'm being honest with myself —and right before you and your poor dog freeze to death from your stupidity seems like to a good time to start being honest—I've spent all the years since leaving home working pretty hard, and succeeding, at feeling as little as possible. *Get lost in your job, upgrade your truck, get yourself a nice place, date casually—always, always casually, nothing more. Trick yourself into believing you're having a great life because it looks good on paper and makes you feel like you've outrun your past.*

But that past was still there, wasn't it? And you've felt it in so many different ways these past few weeks. And deep down, that got you afraid all over again, same as when you were a teenager. It got you afraid of giving a crap about anyone or anything that might pull the rug out from under you.

What I didn't expect, though, was that Dad dying

would have that same effect, even though this time it wasn't his fault and he had no control over the rug.

That's when it hits me that maybe I was wrong about something. Maybe there *was* a miracle for Dad in the end: those last couple of unexpected hours together. Or maybe it was for me. Maybe, like George Bailey, I didn't get the life I was hoping for, but it's full of good things just the same.

Or it was. Before I screwed everything up here.

It's getting colder now and Marley's starting to shiver. I reach under the seat, thankful I've always kept an old blanket there. It's actually a blanket from my childhood—one Dad kept there before me. The reason? "You just never know when you might need it," he told me when I asked him. I'm not sure I've actually ever needed it, in all these years. But I need it now. *Thanks, Dad.*

Pulling the dog over into my lap, I wrap us both in the blanket as best I can, hugging her to me underneath it. "Sorry, girl," I tell her, stroking her fur, trying to comfort us both. "I made a stupid decision."

Stroking her fur in an effort towards warmth, of more than one kind, I hear myself murmur, "I could be with Lexi right now." The words, spoken out loud, seem to summon still more honesty from deep inside me. "I could be curled up with her, warm and safe, letting her help me believe this pain is survivable.

"I could be getting brave enough to think about a future with her. A future where I don't run from things. A future where I finally let go of all my past crap in that town. A future where I'm not alone. And she isn't, either."

Because we both have been. For years. Yeah, she

handled it better than me—she handles *most* things better than me—but she's been left to deal with life on her own, too. How did I miss that up to now? I've spent so much time thinking how different she and I are in so many ways —but the one way we're alike is...we both know what it is to be alone in the world, without family.

I blow out a heavy breath filled with the truth currently barreling through me. "I should be there with her now. And I should be sitting down to Christmas dinner with her and Helen and Dara tomorrow."

I was an idiot to ever even think of leaving her behind. "I, more than most people, know exactly how it feels to be left behind by someone you love—and I still got in this truck and drove away?"

If I had any doubts about my feelings for her, sitting here in a truck half-buried in snow in the middle of nowhere while a blizzard rages on all sides, it's become clear to me.

"I love her, too, Marley. And now she's never gonna know it."

Christmas Day

Lexi

I haven't felt this horrible on Christmas morning since the first one after Mom and Grandma died. But I have a holiday dinner to prepare, and friends to welcome. And as I drag myself to the kitchen just past daybreak to shove the turkey in the oven, I give myself a pep talk. "It's a beautiful Christmas day. You have so much to be thankful for. And as for Travis Hutchins, well...a month ago he was nothing to you but a bad memory. He can go back to being that again now."

It's not that easy, of course. *This* bad memory is new and fresh and cuts deep.

Back in school, I never really knew him. And I'm not sure I would've liked him if I had. But this grown-up Travis was...just what I didn't know I needed in my life. And he made the holidays even happier—for me and all the people who put a wish in that box that came true, with or without our assistance. And because of him, my shop survived the season!

"But he's gone," I remind myself. "And it's time to pull yourself together and make merry, like it or not."

As I pour myself a cup of coffee and pad in my flannel PJs over to plug the Christmas tree lights in, I try to take comfort in the warmth that surrounds me. The lights sparkle, my apartment radiates holiday warmth, and soon it'll be filled with friends. Outside, the snow stopped at some point overnight and a snowplow has come through to make today's travels easier. But there's no denying that this Christmas isn't going to be the one I expected and that my heart hurts for having to endure one more loss: the Grinch I was foolish enough to fall for.

I unlock the shop's front door early so everyone can come in with ease. Helen is the first to arrive, a couple of hours before our other guests—she's helping with the rest of the meal. She arrives at the top of my stairs with a "Knock, knock, and merry Christmas!"

I come to greet her in a blue sweater sporting a big, smiling snowman face, and she's donned a long, green elf sweater, with an elf hat to match.

"Cute!" I tell her, trying to set aside my heartache.

"I'm going to take elfies with everyone for my social media," she announces with her usual grin as she hefts the bags she's toting to the kitchen counter. Then she lets the

The Christmas Box

grin fade to ask, "How's Travis doing? He hasn't answered my calls or texts."

I'm still not sure what's happened—I just hope I can answer without breaking in to tears. "I have no idea how he is because he left. Just got in his truck with Marley last night and went flying out of town without a word to me while I was sitting here waiting for him." I end on a shaky sigh, a little embarrassed because now Helen has to feel sad for me.

Her face falls. "You're kidding. Oh no. That poor boy."

I let my eyes go wide. "Poor boy? What about poor me? I'm the one with the broken heart."

She slips an arm around my shoulder to tell me, "I'm afraid our Travis might just have a broken heart of his own. Tom passed last night, honey. One minute he was sitting up, watching a movie, and talking, and the next he was gone."

I let out a gasp, trying to wrap my head around it. I guess I got caught up in my own issues and forgot about what Travis might be going through.

"Travis rushed out of the manor, upset, but I assumed he was headed straight to you."

I shake my head. "Nope. I watched him drive away in a blizzard."

She blows out a discouraged-sounding breath. "Well, now I'm worried. Let me try him again in case he was just driving and hasn't looked at his phone." She pulls her cell phone from her pocket and taps the screen a few times. A moment later, she says to me, "Still straight to voicemail," then leaves a message. *Travis, it's Helen again. Please call* or text me as soon as you get this. I need to know you're okay."

As Helen and I go about getting ready for the festivities, she tells me more about what happened at the manor last night and I reveal more about my heartbreak. She stops in the middle of mashing potatoes, the old-fashioned way, to give me a big hug.

And I tell her, "Maybe he's fine. He probably made it home and is sleeping in. Maybe he'll call you later. Or, now that his dad's gone, maybe he's just...done with Winterberry and everyone in it and we'll never hear from him again."

Soon, other guests show up. Chuck from the Christmas tree lot brings a neighbor named Dennis who just moved to town, and I'm so grateful that Dennis is a strong, burly guy able to carry Dara's mom up the steps when Dara texts me from the front sidewalk. Elaine Mitts arrives with her usual green bean casserole, and Dean from the post office comes bearing a pecan pie.

And even though my heart is breaking to know what sent Travis barreling out of town, I'm still so hurt—not to mention angry that he let Dara down, too, after he was so insistent on making all those wishes come true. Maybe I never should have asked him to build that box. Maybe he was right all along and it's just a bunch of false hope.

Fortunately, entertaining is a distraction. Christmas music plays, the aroma of good food fills the apartment, and I put on my happy hostess face as Helen and I carry serving dishes to my dining table, everyone gathered around it.

"Chuck, will you carve?" Helen asks our tree-lot friend as she places the turkey platter in the center of the table.

As he takes up the big knife, my heart wilts a little further remembering Travis's cute, funny insistence that he wouldn't carve the roast beast. Guess he meant it, since he's not even here.

That's when I hear a clatter on the wooden stairs and look over—to see Travis walk through the door, Marley on a leash at his feet! They're both wearing Santa hats.

"Am I too late?" he asks, his dark eyes landing on me.

"Travis!" Helen's face lights up as she presses a hand to her chest. "What a relief! And no, you're just in time. We're just sitting down to dinner."

But his gaze stays locked with mine. "That's not exactly what I meant." Everyone continues to stare at him, but he seems to have eyes only for me. "I'm sorry to interrupt, but can I talk to you privately?"

Without replying, I get up and walk into the living room, stopping next to the tree. Like Helen, I'm relieved beyond words to see him alive and well—but I refuse to let it show. Because that doesn't fix my shattered heart.

"I'm sure Helen told you Dad passed away."

I nod, saying, "I'm truly sorry, Travis. I know how hard it is."

"I know you do," he replies. "And...I just didn't handle it with your grace. Instead, I panicked. I thought I was ready for it, but I was wrong. And I guess I started fearing *other* kinds of losses, too. Other things that could fall apart. So I headed for Chicago, a place...well, where it's always felt like nothing could hurt me. Only then I ran out of gas and was stranded on the side of the road with a dead phone in a snowstorm, and that's when I realized...all I wanted was to be with *you*."

I choose not to react. Because this is coming at me fast. I simply ask, "Then what happened?"

He takes a deep breath and tells me, "It was getting cold and I was pretty sure Marley and I were gonna freeze to death, so I did what I thought you would do. I made a wish. I wished really, really hard for some kind of help. Then a few minutes later, I heard the first sound of an approaching vehicle since I ran out of gas, so I jumped out and waved it down. It was a semi-truck, and the woman driving it was kind of...an angel. She took Marley and me to the next exit, we got gas, and she drove us back to the truck and waited to make sure I got going and wasn't stuck. Then I *did* get stuck on the way back—the interstate was closed for a while. But I finally rolled into town a little while ago."

"And?" I guess I'm still waiting for...more. Something that makes it all more than just words, some sort of proof that this is real between me and him.

"And...I brought you this." He holds up a small sparkling red gift bag. "A little late. A *lot* late. I was too dumb in high school to see the opportunity before me. I was too dumb to see it even just a week ago. But I see it now, very clearly." And instead of giving me the bag, he reaches inside it to pull out the most beautiful laurel wreath I've ever seen. Holly berries nestled in pine sprigs glisten with artificial snow and long red velvet ribbons stream down the back I can't hold in my gasp as he places it gently on my head.

I turn toward the mirror hanging above my mantel, unable to hide my awe as I reach up to touch it. "Where on earth did you get this on Christmas day?"

"From Bill at the Holly Leaf," he informs me. "He wasn't too happy about my request, but when he heard it was for you, he agreed to meet me at the floral shop on my way back into town. And..."

"There's more?" I ask, letting my eyes go wide.

"Yeah. Your wish came true." With that, he reaches down to extract a slip of paper from the front pocket of his blue jeans.

And I'm stunned to see my missing wish between his fingers. Taking it from him, reading it once more—*That Travis decides to stay in town, and maybe he even falls in love with me*—I'm crumbling with embarrassment...until I grasp what he just said. That my wish came true. I dare to raise my gaze to his, asking cautiously, "Which one?"

"Both," he tells me. "And this time I'm not going anywhere. You're stuck with me—I promise." After which he leans down to lower a gentle kiss to my lips that leaves me tingling from the top of my head to the tips of my toes. "Merry Christmas," he whispers deeply in my ear. "From your favorite reformed Grinch."

One Year Later
Christmas Eve

Lexi

The tree in my apartment is beautifully lit, the fire blazing, and on TV, George Bailey is begging Clarence the Angel to get him back to the wonderful life he'd taken for granted. Travis and I are snuggling on the couch, Crinkle wrapped in my arms, and Marley is curled up on Travis's other side. All four of us wear matching Christmas pajamas. Tomorrow will be another Christmas dinner with our friends, but tonight is just for us.

The past year has flown by quicker than Santa's sleigh, and so much has happened.

After finishing his work on the soap shop, Travis started his own carpentry business and has more business than he can keep up with. He does off-site projects primarily in his dad's workshop, and on weekends, he's updating his old family home to move into. He still regrets not having more time with his father, but we know his dad would be happy with Travis's plans to stay on the farm. Today, on this first anniversary of losing him, we took poinsettias to his grave.

Meanwhile, the Christmas Box is going strong. As Chet predicted, the profits from last December were needed to sustain us through slow months, but Travis's illegal interstate sign last year taught us that advertising pays off. So Dara has worked to build up a social media following that now draws people from all over the region and beyond. And no one comes in without leaving a wish in the wishing box.

Like last year, Travis and I committed ourselves to making as many wishes come true as we could, and it's a tradition we plan to continue in years to come.

After the movie ends, Travis glances toward the mantel and asks me, "What's that in your stocking?"

Two old-fashioned red velvet stockings with our names embroidered on them flank the fireplace, but they're empty, so I say, "Nothing."

"No," he says, still peering toward the fireplace, "I think I see something peeking out of yours. You'd better go check."

I turn to eye him speculatively. I still don't see anything "peeking" from my stocking. But, even as comfy as I am with my guy, I ease out of the cuddle and walk over to look.

"You're wrong," I say upon reaching it. "There's nothing sticking out of it."

"Hmm. Well, maybe you should reach down inside just to be sure."

What exactly is my handsome ex-Scrooge up to here?

Tossing him another suspicious look, I slide my hand into the stocking—to pull out an adorable little box tied with a lovely red ribbon. "What's this?" I ask, surprised. We agreed to exchange gifts tomorrow morning.

His eyes widen playfully as he tells me, "Open it and see."

Tugging on the ribbon, I pull it free, then lift the small box's lid to find a beautiful diamond ring inside. A gasp leaves me as joy ripples through my heart. And that's when Travis is suddenly up off the couch, too, dropping to one knee in his holiday PJs next to my Christmas tree, taking my hand in his.

"Alexandra Louise Hargrove," he begins, "over the past year, you've made me happier than I knew I could be. You've shown me how to find the good in life, and how to live in the Christmas spirit all year long. I love you. Will you make me the luckiest ex-Grinch in the world and marry me?"

"Of course," I say.

As Travis slips the sparkling ring on my finger, I think about how yet another kind of Christmas box has just brought us even closer, and how one more wish—which I wrote on a wishing box slip a few weeks ago but never put inside, since it turned out that wasn't necessary anyway—has just come true.

More Christmas magic.

Also by Toni Blake

The Box Books

The Wedding Box

The Christmas Box

The Summer Island trilogy

The One Who Stays

The Giving Heart

The Love We Keep

The Rose Brothers trilogy

Brushstrokes

Mistletoe

Heartstrings

The Coral Cove trilogy

All I Want is You

Love Me if You Dare

Take Me All the Way

The Destiny Series

One Reckless Summer

Sugar Creek

Whisper Falls

Holly Lane

Willow Springs

Half Moon Hill

Christmas in Destiny

Return to Destiny

Standalone Novels

Wildest Dreams

The Red Diary

Letters to a Secret Lover

Tempt Me Tonight

Swept Away

The Mandy Project

The Perfect Mistake

The Weekend Wife

The Bewitching Hour

The Guy Next Door

The Cinderella Scheme

About the Author

Toni Blake's love of writing began when she won an essay contest in the fifth grade. Soon after, she penned her first novel, nineteen notebook pages long. Since then, Toni has become a RITA™-nominated author of over thirty contemporary romance novels, her books have received the National Readers' Choice Award and Bookseller's Best Award, and her work has been excerpted in *Cosmo*. Toni lives in the Midwest and enjoys traveling, crafts, and spending time outdoors.

www.toniblake.com

Milton Keynes UK
Ingram Content Group UK Ltd.
UKHW020819231024
450026UK00004B/296